Roland

Roland Topor was born in Paris [...]
Jewish refugees, and was blessed with prodigious creative
talent. He was a prolific painter, cartoonist and short story
writer, and in 1962 was a founder member of 'Groupe
Panique' with Fernando Arrabal, Alexandro Jodorowsky and
Jacques Sternberg; he was later associated with the artistic
movement Fluxus, working closely with such artists as Daniel
Spoerri and Robert Filliou.

Topor acted on stage and film, notably in Werner Herzog's
Nosferatu and Volker Schlöndorff's *Swann in Love,* and
frequently designed for the theatre and for opera, Alfred
Jarry's *Ubu Roi* being a favourite subject. His feature film
Marquis, made with Henri Xonneux and based on the life of
the Marquis de Sade, was released in 1981.

The Tenant was originally published in French as *Le Locataire
Chimérique* and was filmed by Roman Polanski in 1976.
Roland Topor died in Paris in 1997.

The Tenant

Roland Topor

Translated by Francis K. Price
from the French
'Le Locataire Chimérique'

BLACK SPRING PRESS LTD
LONDON
1997

First published in Great Britain by Doubleday & Co Inc, 1966
This edition first published by Black Spring Press Ltd, 1997

© Roland Topor 1966

Translation by Francis K Price
© Doubleday (Bantam Doubleday Dell
Publishing Group Inc), 1966

Black Spring Press Ltd
63 Harlescott Road
London SE15 3DA

ISBN: 0 948238 26 7

A catalogue record for this book is available from the
British Library.

Cover design by Scarlet Scardanelli
Printed and bound in Great Britain by
The Guernsey Press Co Ltd, Guernsey, Channel Islands.

Contents

PART ONE: THE NEW TENANT

1	*The Apartment*	9
2	*The Former Tenant*	17
3	*The Transition*	25
4	*The Neighbours*	33
5	*The Mysteries*	44
6	*The Robbery*	56

PART TWO: THE NEIGHBOURS

7	*The Battle*	71
8	*Stella*	80
9	*The Petition*	90
10	*The Fever*	100
11	*The Revelation*	109

PART THREE: THE FORMER TENANT

12	*Revolt*	119
13	*The Old Trelkovsky*	130
14	*The Siege*	137
15	*Flight*	146
16	*The Accident*	154
17	*The Preparations*	163
18	*The Possessed*	168
	Epilogue	174

PART ONE

THE NEW TENANT

I

The Apartment

Trelkovsky was on the point of being thrown out in the street when his friend Simon told him about an apartment on the rue de Pyrénées. He went to look at it. The concierge, an ill-tempered woman, refused to show it to him, but a thousand franc note changed her mind.

"Follow me," she said then, without altering her surly attitude.

Trelkovsky was an honest, polite young man in his early thirties, and above everything else he detested complications. He earned a modest living, but the prospect of losing the roof over his head was nothing less than a catastrophe, since his salary would not permit the extravagance of living in a hotel. He did, however, have a few savings in the bank, and he was counting on these to pay the under-the-counter fee he knew the landlord would demand. He could only hope it would not be too high.

The apartment consisted of two gloomy rooms, with no kitchen. A single window in the back room looked directly out on an oddly shaped oval window in the wall on the other side of a courtyard. Trelkovsky thought it must be

9

the window of one of the toilets in the building next door. The walls of the apartment had been covered with a yellowish paper on which there were now several large stains, caused by dampness. The whole ceiling seemed covered with a network of tiny cracks, spreading out and crossing each other like the veins of a leaf. Little bits of plaster which had fallen from it crunched beneath their shoes. In the room without a window, a mantelpiece of fake marble framed a small gas heater.

"The tenant who used to live here threw herself out of the window," the concierge said, seeming suddenly to have become more friendly. "Look, you can see where she fell."

She led Trelkovsky through a jumbled labyrinth of furniture to the window, and gestured triumphantly towards the wreckage of a glass roofing over the courtyard, three storeys below.

"She's not dead," she said, "but she might just as well be. She's at the Saint-Antoine hospital."

"And what if she recovers?" Trelkovsky murmured.

"There's no danger of that," the odious woman laughed. "Don't give it a thought." She winked at him, and added, "It's a piece of luck for you."

"What are the conditions?" Trelkovsky asked.

"Reasonable. There's a small fee to be paid, for the water. The plumbing is all new. Before, you had to go out to the landing for running water. The landlord had it done."

"What about the toilets?"

"Just over there. You go down, and then you take the B staircase. From over there you can see the apartment. And vice versa." She winked again, obscenely. "It's a view worth looking at!"

Trelkovsky was far from being overwhelmed with delight. But even as it was, the apartment was a windfall.

"How much is the fee?" he asked.

"Five hundred thousand. The rent is fifteen thousand francs a month."

"That's expensive. I couldn't pay more than four hundred thousand."

"That's not up to me. You'll have to work it out with the landlord." Another wink. "Go and see him. He lives on the floor beneath this, so you won't have to go far. I have to get back now—but don't forget what I told you. It's a chance you don't want to miss."

Trelkovsky followed her down the steps to the landlord's door. He rang the bell, and an old woman opened the door, peering at him suspiciously.

"We don't give anything to the blind," she snapped, before he could say a word.

"It's about the apartment . . ."

A look of cunning narrowed her eyes. "What apartment?"

"The one on the floor above. Could I see Monsieur Zy?"

The old woman left Trelkovsky standing at the door. He heard the murmuring of voices, and then she came back to tell him Monsieur Zy would see him. She led him into the dining-room, where Monsieur Zy was sitting at the table, meticulously picking at his teeth with the sharpened point of a matchstick. With a little gesture of a finger he indicated that he was busy, and went on rummaging among his upper molars. After a moment he withdrew a tiny bit of meat speared on the pick, studied it attentively, then replaced it in his mouth and swallowed it. Only then did he turn his attention to Trelkovsky.

"Have you seen the apartment?" he said.

Trelkovsky nodded. "Yes. That's why I wanted to see you—to discuss the conditions."

"Five hundred thousand, and fifteen thousand a month."

"That's what the concierge told me. But I wanted to know if that is your final price, because I can't pay more than four hundred thousand."

The landlord frowned. For the space of a minute or two, he said nothing, and his eyes followed the movements of the old woman as she cleared off the table. He seemed to be passing in review everything he had just eaten. Occasionally he nodded his head, as if in approval. He returned at last to the subject under discussion.

"The concierge told you about the water?"

"Yes."

"It's damnably hard to find an apartment these days. There's a student who gave me half that much for just one room on the sixth floor. And he doesn't have water."

Trelkovsky coughed, to clear out his throat; he realized that he was frowning too.

"Please understand me," he said. "I'm not trying to belittle your apartment, but after all, there is no kitchen. And the toilets are also a problem ... Just suppose that I should get sick—which I don't very often do, I can assure you of that—and had to relieve myself in the middle of the night ... Well, it wouldn't be very convenient. And on the other hand, even though I only gave you four hundred thousand I would give it to you in cash."

The landlord held up a hand to interrupt him. "It isn't a question of the money. I won't make any bones of that, Monsieur ..."

"Trelkovsky."

"Monsieur Trelkovsky. I'm in no difficulties there. I don't need your money in order to go on eating. No; I am renting because I have a vacant apartment and I know how scarce they are."

"Of course."

"However, there is the principle of the thing. I am not

a miser, but neither am I a philanthropist. Five hundred thousand is the price. I know other landlords who would ask seven hundred thousand, and be within their rights. As for myself, I am asking five hundred thousand and I have no reason to accept less."

Trelkovsky had followed this discourse with little approving nods of the head and a smile of understanding on his lips. "Of course, Monsieur Zy," he said. "I understand your point of view perfectly; it's entirely reasonable. But ... May I offer you a cigarette?" The landlord declined, and Trelkovsky went on, "We are not savages, after all. We can argue these points, but we can always try to understand each other. You want five hundred thousand. Good. But if someone were to give you five hundred thousand spread over a period of three months that three months could turn into three years. Do you think that would be preferable to four hundred thousand in a lump sum?"

"No, I don't. I know better than you that nothing is preferable to the entire sum in cash. But I prefer five hundred thousand cash to four hundred thousand cash."

Trelkovsky lit his cigarette. "Naturally. And I have no intention of saying that you are wrong. But just think for a minute—the former tenant is not yet dead. Perhaps she will come back. And then, perhaps, if she is ill, or can't climb the stairs, she might want to exchange the apartment for something else. And you know that you don't have the legal right to oppose such an exchange. In that case, it isn't four hundred thousand you would have, it would be nothing. But with me—I will give you the four hundred thousand, there will be no complications, and everything will be worked out on a friendly basis. No problems for you, and none for me. Can you think of a better solution than that?"

"You're talking about a highly unlikely eventuality."

"Perhaps, but it is possible. But with the four hundred thousand cash, no problems, no complications . . ."

"Very well—let's forget about that angle of it for a moment, Monsieur . . . Trelkovsky. I've already told you that it isn't the most important consideration for me. Are you married? Excuse me for asking, but it's because of the children. This is a very quiet house; my wife and I are old . . ."

"Not so old as all that, Monsieur Zy!" Trelkovsky interrupted.

"I know what I am saying. We are both old people, and we don't like noise. So I warn you now that if you are married and have children you could offer me a million francs and I wouldn't accept."

"You can stop worrying about that, Monsieur Zy. You won't have that kind of trouble with me. I am very quiet myself, and I am a bachelor."

"Bachelors can be a problem, too. If you want the apartment as a place to entertain your girl friends, then this is not the house for you. I would rather take two hundred thousand and give it to someone who really needed it."

Trelkovsky nodded. "I agree completely. And I am not that kind of person. I'm a quiet man, and I don't like complications. You won't have any with me."

"Don't be offended by all these things I am asking you now." the landlord said. "We might as well understand each other from the first, and then we can live together without disagreement."

"You're perfectly right; it's the only logical thing to do."

"In that case, you must also understand that I can't permit you to have animals here—cats, dogs, or any other kind of animal."

"I don't intend to."

"Well then, Monsieur Trelkovsky—I can't give you an

14

answer yet, of course; there can't be any question of that as long as the former tenant is still alive. But I like you; you give me the impression of being a serious young man. So I will just say this: come back later in the week. At that time, I should be in a position to give you a definite reply."

Trelkovsky thanked him profusely before leaving. As he passed in front of the concierge's room, she glanced at him curiously, without the slightest sign of recognition, and went back to the interrupted routine of drying a plate with the skirt of her apron.

He paused on the street to study the outside of the building. The upper floors were bathed in the light of the September sun, giving it the appearance of being almost new and fresh. He looked for the window of "his" apartment, but immediately remembered that it looked out on the courtyard.

The whole of the fifth floor had been repainted pink, with the shutters in a canary yellow. The harmony was not subtle, but the note of colour it gave to the building had a happy sound. There were boxes of green plants all along the windows of the third floor, and on the fourth, grilles had been added to heighten the support rail of the balcony—because of children, perhaps, although that did not seem likely, since the landlord did not want children. The roof was studded with chimneys of every size and shape. A cat, which certainly did not belong to any of the tenants, was strolling among them. Trelkovsky smiled to himself, imagining that it was he who was up there, instead of the cat, being gently warmed by the rays of the sun. But then he noticed a curtain moving on the second floor, in the landlord's apartment, and walked hastily away.

The street was almost deserted, doubtless because it was still the lunch hour. Trelkovsky stopped and bought himself some bread and a few slices of garlic sausage. He sat down on a bench and considered matters as he ate.

After all, perhaps the argument he had used with the landlord was correct, and the former tenant would come back and want to exchange the apartment. Perhaps she would recover. He sincerely hoped she would, of course. But if she didn't, perhaps she had left a will. In that case, what were the landlord's rights in the matter? Would Trelkovsky be obliged to pay the fee twice—once to the landlord, and again to the former tenant? He wished that he could talk to his friend Scope, who was a lawyer's clerk, but unfortunately he was out of town on some sort of business.

"The best thing to do is to go and see the former tenant in the hospital," he thought.

As soon as he had finished eating, he went back to the building to question the concierge. She informed him, with ill-concealed bad temper, that the tenant's name was Mademoiselle Choule.

"Poor woman!" Trelkovsky said, and wrote the name down on the back of an envelope.

2

The Former Tenant

The next day, at precisely the prescribed visiting hour, Trelkovsky entered the door of the Saint-Antoine hospital. He was wearing his only dark suit, and in his right hand he carried a pound of oranges wrapped in an old newspaper.

He had always had a very unhappy reaction to hospitals. It seemed to him that he could hear a final rasping breath behind every window, and that the instant he turned his back they would begin moving out the corpses. He considered both doctors and nurses to be monsters of insensitivity, in spite of the fact that he admired their devotion to duty.

At the information window, he asked where he might find Mademoiselle Choule. The young woman on duty consulted her cards.

"Are you a member of the family?" she asked.

Trelkovsky hesitated. If he answered in the negative, would they just send him away? Finally, he said, "I'm a friend."

"Ward 27, bed 18. See the chief nurse first."

He murmured a word of thanks and went in. Ward 27 was enormous, as big as the main lobby of a railway station. Four rows of beds stretched down its entire length. Around the white shapes of the beds clustered little groups of people whose sombre clothing formed a startling contrast. It was the rush hour for visitors. A continuous murmuring, like the roar of the sea imprisoned in a shell, drummed at his ears. A woman in white snatched at his arm and thrust out her jaw aggressively.

"What are you doing here?" she demanded.

"Are you the chief nurse?" Trelkovsky asked, and when the jaw nodded he said, "My name is Trelkovsky. I'm very glad I found you, because I was told at the information desk to see you first. It's about Mademoiselle Choule."

"Bed 18?"

"That's what I was told. May I see her?"

The chief nurse frowned, put a pencil between her teeth, and chewed on it thoughtfully before answering.

"She can't be disturbed," she said at last. "She was in a coma until yesterday. Go ahead, but be very careful, and don't try to talk to her."

Trelkovsky had no great trouble finding bed 18. A woman was stretched out in it, her face covered with bandages, and her left leg suspended by a complicated system of pulleys. The single eye visible through the bandages was open. Trelkovsky approached the bed very quietly. He could not tell whether the woman had noticed him, because the eye did not blink, and she was so heavily bandaged that he could see nothing of the expression on her face. He put the oranges on the bed table and sat down on a little stool.

She seemed older than he had thought she would be. She was breathing with great difficulty, her mouth wide open, like a black veil in the centre of a white field. He noticed, with an acute sense of embarrassment, that one of her upper incisor teeth was missing.

"Are you one of her friends?"

He jumped, involuntarily. He hadn't noticed the other visitor. His forehead, which was already damp, broke out in little pearls of sweat. He imagined himself in the place of a guilty man about to be denounced by a witness he had forgotten. All sorts of insane explanations flashed through his mind. But the other visitor, a young girl, was already talking again.

"What on earth could have happened? Do you know why she did a thing like this? At first, I just wouldn't believe it. When I think that I saw her the night before, and she was in such good spirits! What could have happened to her?"

Trelkovsky breathed a sigh of relief. The girl had obviously classified him at once as a member of Mademoiselle Choule's large circle of friends. She wasn't really asking him a question; she was simply stating her position. He studied her more closely.

She was pleasant to look at, because without being pretty she was exciting. She was the sort of girl Trelkovsky conjured up in his imagination during the most private moments of his life. Insofar as the body was concerned at least—a body which could perfectly easily have done without a head—it was well-rounded, but without softness or fat.

The girl was wearing a green sweater which threw the line of her breasts into sharp relief, and because of her brassière—or the absence of a brassière—he could distinguish the point of the nipples. Her navy-blue skirt had climbed to a point well above her knees, but this was the result of negligence, not calculation. The fact remained that a considerable portion of flesh was visible beneath the elastic strap that held her stocking. This milky, shadowed flesh of the thigh, extraordinarily luminous just before it dipped to the sombre regions at the centre, hypnotised Trelkovsky. He had difficulty detaching his gaze from it and looking up again at the girl's face, which was absolutely commonplace. Chestnut hair, vaguely chestnut eyes, a large mouth awkwardly disguised with lipstick.

"To tell you the truth," he began, after having cleared his throat, "I'm not really a friend. I scarcely knew her." Modesty forbade him from admitting that he didn't know her at all. "But believe me, I'm terribly sad and upset about what happened."

The girl smiled at him. "Yes, it's terrible."

She turned her attention back to the prostrate figure on the bed, which seemed still to be unconscious, in spite of the one open eye.

"Simone, Simone," the girl murmured, "you recognize me, don't you? It's Stella; your friend, Stella. Don't you recognize me?"

The eye remained steadily fixed, contemplating some invisible point on the ceiling. Trelkovsky wondered if she might not be dead, but just then a moaning sound came from the mouth, stifled at first, then swelling to an unbearable scream.

Stella began to weep noisily, embarrassing Trelkovsky enormously. He was tempted to say "Ssh!" in her ear, because he was certain that everyone in the room was looking at them, thinking he was responsible for her tears. He glanced furtively at their nearest neighbours to see how they were reacting. On his left an old man was sleeping, his body twitching constantly beneath the covers. His lips mouthed a flow of unintelligible words, while his jaw moved rhythmically up and down, as though he were sucking on a giant bit of candy. A thread of blood-tinged saliva ran down the side of his face to disappear in the whiteness of the sheet. On the right, a fat, alcoholic peasant stared in wonderment at the food and wine being unpacked by the group of visitors around his bed. Trelkovsky was relieved to see that no one was paying any attention to Stella and himself. A few minutes later, a nurse came up to tell them that they must leave now.

"Is there any chance of saving her?" Stella asked. She was still weeping, but only intermittently.

The nurse glanced at her irritably. "What do you think?" she demanded. "If we can save her we will. What more do you want to know?"

"But what do you think?" Stella said. "Is it possible?"

The nurse lifted her shoulders in annoyance. "Ask the doctor; he won't tell you any more than I just have. In this kind of thing ..." Her voice assumed a tone of importance, "... no one can really say. The fact that she came out of the coma is enough for now!"

Trelkovsky felt vaguely let down. He had not been able to talk with Simone Choule, and the fact that the poor woman had one foot in the grave did nothing to comfort him. He was not a selfish or an evil young man, and he would honestly have preferred to remain in his present unhappy situation, if by doing so he could have saved her.

"I'm going to talk to this Stella," he thought. "Perhaps she can tell me some of the things I don't know."

But he had no idea how to strike up a conversation, because the girl persisted in weeping. It was difficult to bring up the subject of the apartment without first having prepared the ground. On the other hand, he was very much afraid that the moment they left the hospital she would hold out her hand and say good-bye, before he had had a chance to decide what to do. And as if this were not bad enough, a sudden, violent need to urinate made it impossible for him to entertain a coherent thought.

He forced himself to walk slowly, in spite of the fact that all he wanted to do was race breathlessly to the nearest toilet.

At last, he summoned up courage to attack the problem. "You mustn't give in to your grief," he said, as calmly as possible. "If you like, we could go and have something to drink. I think it would help you."

Then he bit his lips until they bled. His need was becoming monstrous, intolerable.

She tried to answer, but a sort of hiccup cut through the words. She gave him a sad little smile, and her head bobbed in a gesture of acceptance.

The sweat was pouring from Trelkovsky's forehead like rain. Need punched at his belly like a strong man's fist. But they had left the hospital now, and there was a large café just across the street.

"Shall we go over there?" he suggested, with poorly feigned indifference.

"If you like," Stella said.

He waited until they had found a table and their order was taken, before saying, "Excuse me for just a minute, please. There's a telephone call I have to make."

When he came back, he was a new man. He felt like laughing and singing, both at once. It was only when he saw Stella's face again, still moist with tears, that he remembered to take on an appearance of concern.

They stirred idly at the glasses the waiter had brought them, but said nothing. Stella was gradually becoming calmer. He watched her carefully, waiting for the psychological moment when he might bring up the matter of the apartment. He also looked at her breasts again, and at that moment he was sure that he would go to bed with her. Finally, he summoned up strength enough to speak.

"I will never understand suicide," he said, gravely. "I

22

have no argument against it, but it's beyond my comprehension. Had you ever discussed it—with her?"

She told him that they had never talked about it, that she had known Simone for a very long time, but that she knew of absolutely nothing in her life that could have explained such an act. Trelkovsky suggested that it might, perhaps, have been the result of a disappointment in love, but Stella was sure that it was not. She knew of no serious relationship at all. Ever since Simone had come to Paris— her parents were in Tours—she had lived almost alone, seeing only a few friends. She had two or three affairs, of course, but without consequence. Simone spent most of her leisure time reading historical novels. She worked in a bookshop.

There was nothing in all of this information that could be considered an obstacle to Trelkovsky's future. He was angry with himself because this pleased him. It seemed almost inhuman. To punish himself, he thought back to this woman who had tried to kill herself.

"Perhaps she will pull out of it," he said, but without conviction.

Stella shook her head. "I don't think so. Did you notice? She didn't even recognize me. I still can't get over that. What a tragedy! I know I won't be able to work this afternoon. I'm just going to stay alone at home and have a fit of the blues."

Trelkovsky did not have to go to work either. He had asked his department head for a few days off while he looked for an apartment.

"That won't do any good," he said. "On the contrary, what you should try to do is take your mind off it completely. It may sound like very bad taste, but what I would advise you to do is to go to a cinema." He paused, and then added hastily, "Perhaps ... if you will permit me ...

I have nothing to do this afternoon myself. Would you like to have lunch with me? We could go to see a film afterwards. If you have nothing else to do . . ."

She accepted.

After lunch in a nearby cafeteria, they went into the first cinema they saw. They were scarcely seated, and the film itself had not yet begun, when he felt her leg pressed tightly against his own. He would have to answer her in some way! He was unable to make up his mind what to do, but he knew he could not just sit there and do nothing. He put his arm around her shoulders. She gave no sign that she had noticed, and after a moment or two he developed a violent cramp in the upper part of his arm. He was still sitting in this uncomfortable position when the lights went on for the interval before the film. He dared not look at Stella. She pressed her thigh even harder against his.

As soon as the cinema was again in darkness, he lifted his arm from her shoulder and passed it around her waist. The tips of his fingers were touching the first swelling of her breast, of that breast he had seen earlier, in the hospital, beneath the taut sheath of the green sweater. She made no attempt to rebuff him. His hand moved up beneath the sweater, coming at last to the brassière, and he managed to slip it between the breast and its envelope of nylon. He could feel the thickness of the nipple beneath his index finger, and began to rotate it slowly back and forth.

She let out a little gasp, and wriggled abruptly in her seat, freeing the breasts entirely from the restriction of the brassière. They were soft and warm. He moulded his hand to them convulsively.

And even as he did so, he thought back to Simone Choule: perhaps she is dying, right at this very moment.

But as it happened, she didn't die until a little later, just about sunset.

24

3

The Transition

Trelkovsky telephoned the hospital from a public booth to inquire about the condition of the former tenant. He was told that she was dead.

He was deeply moved by this brutish ending. It was as if he had just lost someone who was very dear to him. He experienced a sudden, heartfelt regret that he had not known Simone Choule in an earlier, better time. They might have gone to films together, to restaurants, shared moments of happiness that she had never known. When he thought of her, Trelkovsky no longer saw her as she had been in the hospital, but imagined her as a very young girl, weeping over some youthful peccadillo. It was at such moments that he would have liked to be with her, to point out to her that, after all, it was simply a peccadillo, that she was wrong to weep, that she should be happy. Because, he would have explained, you won't live very long, you will die some night in a room in a hospital, without ever having lived.

"I'll go to the funeral. It's the least I can do. I'll probably see Stella there . . ."

He had, in fact, left Stella without even asking for her address. When they left the cinema they had looked at each other awkwardly, without finding anything to say. The circumstances under which they met had caused a vague sense of remorse. For his part, Trelkovsky had only one consuming desire: to flee, at once. They had parted company after a purely perfunctory assurance that they would see each other again.

At the moment, his feeling of solitude made him regret that he had not taken advantage of this occasion to escape from it. And for all he knew, she felt the same way.

There was no funeral. The body was to be sent to her home in Tours, to be buried there. A Mass would be held in the church of Menilmontant. Trelkovsky decided to attend.

The service had already begun when he entered the church. He sat down very quietly on the first chair he came to and glanced around him at the other participants. There were very few. He recognized the back of Stella's head in the first row, but she did not turn around. He set his mind to passing the time.

He had never been a religious person himself, but he respected the beliefs of others. He was careful now to imitate their movements and their attitudes, to kneel at the proper times, and to rise when they did. But the mournful atmosphere surrounding him gradually took possession of his thoughts. He was overwhelmed by a succession of gloomy speculations. Death itself was present in the church, and he was more conscious of this presence than of any other.

Trelkovsky was not in the habit of thinking very much about death. It was not that he was indifferent to it—far from it—but precisely for that reason he systematically avoided thinking about it. Whenever he became aware that his thoughts were drifting into this dangerous area he brought out the arsenal of evasive weapons he had built up and perfected over the years. In such critical moments, for example, he might begin singing aloud some of the catchy, foolish airs he had heard on the radio, since they provided a perfect barrier to any kind of thought. If this should fail, he occasionally pinched himself until he bled, or took refuge in erotic fantasies. He called up a picture of a woman he had seen in the street, bending over to adjust her stocking; of a bust whose outlines he had traced beneath the blouse of a saleswoman; of some dimly remembered spectacle he had stumbled on by chance. That was the bait. If his mind bit at it, his imagination then took over and its power was enormous. It lifted the skirts, tore off the blouses, altered and expanded the memories. And little by little, in the presence of swooning women and writhing flesh, the image of death became less clear, faded into the distance, and eventually vanished completely, like a vampire at the first light of dawn.

This time, however, the image would not recede. For one second of terrifying intensity Trelkovsky had an absolute physical sense of the gulf above which he stood. He was seized with dizziness. And then came all the horrible details: the nails being driven into the coffin, the earth falling heavily against its walls and top, the slow decomposition of the corpse.

He struggled to gain control of himself, and failed. He knew that he would have to scratch at his own body before he could be sure that the worms did not exist, did not yet exist. He did it discreetly at first, and then furiously, unable to shake off the sensation of thousands of hideous little animals gnawing at his flesh, boring their way into his entrails. He began humming a stupid tune to himself, but that did no good and he could not sing aloud here.

As a last recourse, he determined to concentrate on death itself. If he could succeed in symbolising death, it would be a manner of escaping it, of getting away. Trelkovsky threw himself wholeheartedly into the game, and finally arrived at a personification which pleased him. This is what he invented:

Death was the Earth. Having sprung from her, the budding forms of life attempted to liberate themselves from her embrace. They set their sights on the free and open spaces. Death let them do as they wished, because she was very partial to the idea of life. She contented herself with keeping a watchful eye on her flock, and when she felt that they were fully ripe she devoured them up as if they were so many morsels of sugar. Then she lay back and slowly digested the nourishment that would replenish her womb, happy and satiated as a pampered cat.

Trelkovsky shook himself violently. He could stand no more of this ridiculous and interminable ceremony. In addition to everything else, it was terribly cold; he was so numb that his sinus ached.

"The devil with Stella, I'm leaving."

He stood up carefully, trying not to make any noise. When he reached the door and turned the handle, nothing happened. Seized with panic he twisted the handle in every possible direction, but in vain. Nothing whatever happened. He no longer dared return to his place, he was even afraid to turn around since he would have to face the disapproving glances he could feel stabbing at his back. He struggled desperately with the door, not understanding the cause of its resistance, rapidly losing hope. It was some time before he noticed the little door cut into the great one, even though it was just a foot or so to his right. It opened with no difficulty, and with a single leap he was outside. He had the feeling of having awakened from a nightmare.

"Monsieur Zy should be able to give me an answer by now," he thought, and set off at once to see the landlord.

The air was soft and warm after the cavernous cold of the church. Trelkovsky suddenly felt so happy that he began to laugh to himself. "After all," he thought, "I'm not dead yet, and before I come to it science will have made such progress that I'll live to be two hundred!"

He had gas on his stomach and, like a child, he began to amuse himself by breaking wind at every step and glancing out of the corner of his eye at the people walking behind him. But an elderly, well-dressed man stared back at him severely and frowned, causing him to go scarlet with embarrassment and removing all desire to go on with his foolish game.

It was Monsieur Zy, in person, who opened the door for him.

"Ah, so it's you again," he said.

"Good afternoon, Monsieur Zy. I see that you recognize me."

"Yes, of course. You came about the apartment? You're interested in it, but you still don't want to put up the price, is that it? You think that I'm the one who is going to give in."

"You have no need to give in, Monsieur Zy," Trelkovsky said hurriedly. "I'll give you your four hundred thousand right away, in cash."

"But I wanted five hundred thousand!"

"We don't always get everything we want, Monsieur Zy. For myself, I would have liked to have the toilets on the same floor but they are not there."

The landlord burst out laughing. A vast, mucous laughter which almost drowned out Trelkovsky's timid echo.

"You're a clever one, aren't you?" he said at last. "All right then, let's say four hundred and fifty thousand cash, and we won't talk about it any more. I'll draw up the lease for you tomorrow. Now are you satisfied?"

Trelkovsky stammered thanks, and then said, "When will I be able to move into the apartment?"

"Right away, if you want to—on condition that you give me an advance on the fee. It's not that I don't trust you, but after all I don't know you, do I? In my business, if I were to trust everyone who came along I wouldn't get very far. Put yourself in my place."

"But it's perfectly natural!" Trelkovsky protested. "I'll bring some of my things tomorrow."

"As you like. You can see that no one has any trouble getting along with me, so long as he behaves properly and pays the rent regularly." The landlord paused briefly, and then added, as if he were imparting a confidence, "It's not a bad thing you've got here, you know. The family has informed me that they don't intend to send for the furniture, so it will all be yours. That's something you certainly didn't expect. The whole amount of my fee wouldn't have paid for that."

"Oh," Trelkovsky shrugged, "a few chairs, a table, a bed and a chest of drawers . . ."

"You think so? Well just go out and buy them and come back and tell me what you found. No—believe me, you've got a good thing here. And you know it very well!"

"I'm very grateful to you, Monsieur Zy," Trelkovsky murmured humbly.

"Oh, gratitude!" Monsieur Zy laughed loudly again, and pushed Trelkovsky back onto the landing, closing the door in his face.

"Good-bye, Monsieur Zy," Trelkovsky shouted, but there was no reply. He waited a moment or two longer and then slowly walked down the stairs.

When he returned to his old studio room, a vast weariness overcame him. He stretched out on the bed, without even taking off his shoes and remained there for a long time with his eyes half closed, just looking around him.

He had lived so many years in this room that he could still not quite grasp the idea that now it was finished. He would never again see this place which had been the very centre of his life. Others would come into it, destroy the order of things that existed now, transform these four walls into something he would not even recognize, and kill off forever any lingering assumption that a certain Monsieur Trelkovsky had lived here before. Unceremoniously, from one day to the next, he would have vanished.

Even now he no longer felt really at home in this room. The uncertainty of his situation had intruded on his last days here. It was like the final minutes spent in a compartment on a train, when you knew that you would arrive in the station at any moment. He had given up such concerns as cleaning and dusting, filing his papers, or even making his bed. The result had not been a state of wild disorder—his possessions were too few to cause that—but an atmosphere of vacancy, of a suddenly cancelled departure.

Trelkovsky slept uninterruptedly until early morning. He set to work then gathering together all his personal belongings, which he had no trouble packing into his two suitcases. He handed in the key to the concierge, and took a taxi to his new address.

He spent the rest of the morning withdrawing his money from the savings bank and concluding the necessary formalities with the landlord.

At noon, he turned the key in the lock of the apartment for the first time. He set the two suitcases just inside the door, but did not go in. He went down the stairs again, and out to a restaurant, because he had eaten nothing since luncheon of the day before.

After lunch, he telephoned his department head to say that he would be back at work the next day.

The period of transition had ended.

4

The Neighbours

Towards the middle of October, after repeated exhortations from his friends—notably Scope, the lawyer's clerk, and Simon, the household appliance salesman—Trelkovsky organized a small party as a sort of house-warming. Some of his friends from the office were also invited, and all the available young girls. The party took place on a Saturday night, so that they could relax and enjoy themselves without worrying about the morning to come.

Everyone had brought something to eat or drink, and all these provisions were scattered across the surface of the table. Trelkovsky had difficulty finding chairs for so many people, but it finally occurred to him to pull the bed up next to the table, and some of the guests then settled down there, to the accompaniment of laughter from the girls and double-edged pleasantries from the men.

If the truth be told, the apartment had never before been so pleasant, and had never seemed so brightly lit. Trelkovsky was deeply moved at the thought of being the beneficiary of all this. Like the apartment itself, he had never before been the object of so much attention. Everyone was silent when he told a story, they laughed when it was funny, and they even applauded. But above everything else, he heard his name being spoken constantly. Someone would say, "I was with Trelkovsky ..." or, "The other day, Trelkovsky ..." or "Trelkovsky was saying ..." He was really king for the time.

Trelkovsky could not take much to drink, but in order to be sure that he would not spoil the pleasure of the others he drank more than they did. The number of empty bottles grew steadily larger, and the girls went right on murmuring encouragement to the drinkers. Someone suggested that the light in this room was too harsh and it would be a good idea to turn it out and switch on the one in the adjoining room, leaving the door open. After that, everyone collapsed on the bed. Trelkovsky could very easily have fallen asleep in this twilight light, but the proximity of so many females, plus the fact that he was beginning to have a headache, kept him awake.

A discussion began between Scope and Simon, on the subject of which was best for a holiday—the seaside or the mountains.

"The mountains, of course," Simon said, in a voice that was more than a trifle thick. "That's the most beautiful thing in all the world. The landscapes! The lakes! The forests! And the air is so pure—nothing like it is in the city. You can walk for miles if you like, or you can climb. When I'm in the mountains, I get up at five o'clock in the morning, I have a cold meal, and then I go out for the whole day, with my pack on my back. I tell you, just being by yourself up there, thousands of feet in the sky, with a magnificent view spread out at your feet—that's the most wonderful feeling I know."

Scope laughed. "Not for me! Every winter—and every summer, too—you hear stories about people falling off cliffs, being buried in avalanches, or stalled for days in a cable car."

"The same thing is true of the seaside," Simon answered. "There are always people being drowned. Every time you turned on the radio this summer there was another one."

"There's no connection between the two. People who drown are just idiots who want to show off and swim out too far."

"It's exactly the same thing in the mountains. They go off alone, without proper preparations, or without train-ing . . ."

Little by little, everyone began to take part in the argu-ment. Trelkovsky said that he had no particular preference, but it did seem to him that the mountains were healthier than the seaside. Some others echoed his opinion, adding their own modifications, and eventually turning it around completely.

Trelkovsky listened absent-mindedly. He was concentra-ting much more intensely on a girl at the other end of the bed. She was lying back in a half-reclining position, remov-ing her shoes without using her hands at all, pushing against the heel of the right shoe with the toe of the left. When it finally fell to the floor, the nylon-sheathed toes of her right foot attacked the left heel, plucking at it stubbornly until it too fell off. Then the girl turned over on her side, pulled her knees up against her chest, and remained abso-utely motionless.

Trelkovsky tried to make out whether she was pretty, but did not succeed. He did notice, however, that she was moving again. Thrusting her legs out straight, then drawing them back against her chest, almost as though she were swimming, she was gradually drawing closer to him. Too dazed by wine and the ache in his head to make a move, he simply watched her in astonishment.

Snatches of the conversation around him occasionally reached his ears, seeming to come from a great distance.

"Oh, no, you're wrong ... the sea ... humid ... more moderate climate."

"I beg your pardon ... oxygen ... two years ago ... with some friends ..."

"Bulls ... cows ... fishing ... sickness ... death ..."

"Let's change the subject ..."

The girl rested her head on Trelkovsky's knees and remained there. Almost automatically, he began to amuse himself by rolling strands of her hair around his fingers.

Why me? he thought. All of a sudden, fortune is smiling at me and instead of taking advantage of it I have a headache. What an idiot I am.

Losing patience with him at last, the girl seized Trelkovsky's hand in a determined grip and placed it firmly over her left breast.

What next? Trelkovsky thought, and decided on the spur of the moment that it would be very clever on his part to make no move at all.

Confronted with the failure of her efforts, the girl pulled herself up a little further, so that she could rest the back of her head on Trelkovsky's chest. She then began rubbing her head back and forth, in the hope of exciting him, but when he remained obstinately motionless she started pinching the flesh of his thigh through his trousers. With lordly indifference, Trelkovsky simply allowed himself to be enticed, smiling haughtily. What could the poor little fool want? To seduce him? Why him, of all people?

He started abruptly, and leaped to his feet, pushing the girl's head away almost angrily. Now he understood. It was his apartment that interested her. He recognized her now. Her name was Lucille. She had come with Albert, who had told him that she was just divorced. The husband

36

had kept the apartment. So that was it—he was being courted for his apartment!

Trelkovsky burst out laughing. In order to hear each other in the midst of the general hubbub, the defenders of the seaside and the mountains were forced to raise their voices. The girl on the bed began to sob. It was at that moment that someone knocked on the door.

Instantly sober, Trelkovsky went to open it.

A man was standing on the landing. He was tall, thin —very thin—and abnormally pale. He was wearing a long, dark red bathrobe.

"Monsieur . . . ?" Trelkovsky murmured.

"You are making a great deal of noise, monsieur," the man said, in a threatening tone. "It's after one o'clock in the morning and you are making a great deal of noise."

"But, monsieur," Trelkovsky said, "it's just a few friends . . . we were talking quietly . . ."

"Quietly?" The man was indignant, and his voice rose proportionately. "I live up above you and I can hear every word you are saying. You drag chairs around, and you walk up and down, making a dreadful racket with your shoes. It's insufferable. Do you intend to carry on like this much longer?"

He was almost shouting now, and Trelkovsky was tempted to tell him that he was the one who was waking up everyone else. But that was doubtless exactly what he would have liked: to attract the attention of the entire building to Trelkovsky's behaviour.

An old woman, tightly wrapped in a dressing gown, was standing on the staircase that led to the fourth floor, leaning forward in an attempt to observe the scene in the doorway.

"Look, monsieur," Trelkovsky said hastily, "I'm terribly

sorry if we woke you. I'm very embarrassed. I assure you
that we'll be more careful . . ."

The man was not to be appeased. "What kind of
business is this, waking people up at one o'clock in the
morning? What kind of manners is that?"

"We'll be careful," Trelkovsky repeated, raising his own
voice a trifle, "but you should . . ."

"I've never seen such a thing! I've never heard such a
row before! Don't you give a damn about anyone else?
It's all very well to amuse yourselves, but there are some
people who have to work!"

"Tomorrow is Sunday. I don't see any reason why I
can't have a few friends on Saturday night."

"Even on Saturday night, monsieur, there is no excuse
for such a racket as this!"

"We'll be more careful," Trelkovsky muttered again, and
closed the door.

He could still hear the other man grumbling, and then
apparently talking to the old woman, since a feminine
voice answered. After two or three minutes however,
silence returned.

Trelkovsky put a hand against his heart and found that
it was beating at twice its normal speed. A cold sweat
beaded his forehead.

His friends, momentarily silenced by the appearance of
the man at the door, began arguing among themselves
again. Everyone wanted to voice an opinion on neighbours
like that. They told stories of friends who had had to put
up with the same sort of problem, and of what they had
done about it. Little by little, they arrived at a discussion
of the best means to combat such annoyances. Then, from
literal methods they passed to imaginary ones, which were
vastly more effective. One highly satisfactory solution was
to bore a hole in the ceiling and introduce a host of venom-

ous spiders or scorpions into the apartment above. They all laughed boisterously at this.

Trelkovsky was in agony. Every time they raised their voices, he went "Ssh!" so violently that they began to make fun of him and laugh and talk even louder, in a deliberate attempt to provoke him. By this time he detested them all to such an extent that he no longer gave the slightest thought to his manners as their host.

He went to get their coats from the other room, handed them out without caring who got whose, and then almost pushed them out on the landing. By way of revenge, they made as much noise as possible all the way down the stairs and never ceased laughing at the fact that he should be so upset. He would have taken great pleasure in pouring boiling oil down the stairwell on their heads. He went back into the apartment and locked the door behind him. As he turned around, he brushed an empty bottle on the table with his elbow. It shattered on the floor with a sound like a gunshot. The consequence was not long in coming— there was a violent pounding from the ceiling beneath. The landlord!

Trelkovsky was ashamed; so deeply ashamed that he felt as if he were blushing from head to toe. He was ashamed of himself and of everything he had done. He was an odious person. The indescribable din of his revelry had roused everyone in the building! Could it be that he had no respect for the rights of others? That he was incapable of living in a normal, civilized society? He felt like sitting down and weeping. What could he possibly say in his own defence? And how, for that matter, could he plead his case against the unanswerable testimony of the pounding on his floor? How could he say, "Yes, I'm guilty, I admit that, but there were extenuating circumstances?"

He didn't have the strength to attempt putting the apartment back in order. He could picture the neighbours only too clearly, listening and waiting for the slightest pretext to pound on his ceiling or his floor. He took off his shoes right where he stood, and crept silently across the room to turn out the light. Then he felt his way back through the darkness, his fingers exploring the space in front of him to avoid any noisy collision with the furniture, and collapsed on the bed.

Tomorrow he would have to confront the neighbours. Would he have the courage for it? Simply thinking about it now, he could feel his strength draining away. What could he say if the landlord demanded an explanation?

He was furious with himself. The stupidity of having organized such a party in his apartment! It was the best means he could have thought of to lose it. He hadn't enjoyed himself, he had spent a good deal of money, and on top of that he had jeopardised his entire future. He had alienated everyone in the building. A splendid beginning!

With this whirling through his head, he finally managed to get to sleep.

The fear of encountering some of his irritated neighbours kept him rooted in the apartment all of Sunday morning. But for that matter, he was far from being consumed with energy. Even the roots of his hair seemed to be sore. He had the feeling that his eyes might drop out of their sockets if he so much as glanced around.

The apartment had an air of almost blasé desolation, offering him a cynical review of the seamy side of the evening. Wreckage littered its every corner, like the sodden objects deposited by the waves on a beach, and left behind when the tide goes out: empty bottles, ashes swimming in the dregs of coffee at the bottom of a cup, bits of a broken plate, limp slices of cold meat ground into the floor by careless heels, glasses stained with a thick sauce of red wine and butts of cigarettes.

Trelkovsky did his best to clean things up, but he found himself at the end with an overflowing pail of refuse. The thought of taking it down before nightfall terrified him; until then, he would just have to tolerate the stale and nauseating smell, mercilessly reminding him of what he had done, with every breath he drew.

He realized at last that he could not do it. Even a battle with the neighbours was preferable to this. He made a valiant effort to whistle as he went down the stairs. Certainly no one would dare rebuke him if they were to see him in such a gay and confident mood. Unhappily, however, he arrived on the second floor landing at the precise moment Monsieur Zy opened his door to go out. It was impossible for Trelkovsky to turn back.

"Good afternoon, Monsieur Zy," he said hastily. "What a beautiful day!" Then, lowering his voice to a confidential whisper, "I'm terribly sorry about last night, Monsieur Zy, I give you my word that nothing of that sort will ever happen again."

The landlord glanced at him coldly. "I should hope not. You woke up both my wife and me, and we couldn't sleep for the rest of the night. And all of your neighbours have complained. What was the meaning of all that?"

"We were celebrating ..." Trelkovsky hesitated. "... my enormous good fortune in having found this splendid apartment. Just a few friends and myself—we thought we could have a kind of—well—a kind of house-warming, without bothering anyone else. Yes, that was it—it was just to be a little house-warming celebration. But you know how things happen—with the best will in the world, and never dreaming of disturbing anyone else, you get to talking, you're having a good time ... And then everyone starts talking at once, and before you know it you're talking louder than you should ... But I'm terribly sorry about it, and I assure you it will never happen again."

The landlord looked Trelkovsky straight in the eyes now. "I'm glad you told me that, Monsieur Trelkovsky, and I hope you mean it, because if not ... I don't mind telling you that I was thinking seriously of taking steps to correct the situation. Very serious steps. I cannot permit a tenant to come into my building and spread disorder and confusion; I cannot permit it. So—we'll forget about it this time, but it is once too often. Don't let it happen again. Apartments are hard enough to find these days, without being foolish enough to lose the one you have. Just remember that."

In the days that followed, Trelkovsky was careful to furnish his neighbours with no pretext whatever for complaint. His radio was always turned down as low as he could get it, and at ten o'clock at night he got into bed and read. In future, he would be able to go down the stairs with his head held high; he was now a full-fledged tenant, or almost so. But he could not escape the feeling that, in spite of his present behaviour, he had not yet been forgiven for the regrettable incident of the party.

Although he seldom saw any of his neighbours, he did occasionally pass someone on the staircase. He had no way of knowing, of course, whether it was a genuine neighbour, or a visiting relative or friend of a neighbour, or simply a door-to-door salesman of some kind. But rather than run the risk of seeming impolite he said good morning to everyone he saw. If he were wearing a hat, he would lift it and bow slightly, and if he were not wearing one his hand would sketch the movement of lifting it. He always moved to the side of the stairway or the landing as soon as he saw anyone approach, and then smiled broadly and waved, saying, "After you, Monsieur" (or Madame, as the case required).

In the same manner, he never failed to say good morning or good evening to the concierge when he saw her, but for her part she continued to return his greeting with a blank stare which contained not the slightest sign of recognition. She invariably just studied him curiously, as if she were surprised every time she saw him. But apart from such brief encounters on the stairs Trelkovsky had no contact at all with his neighbours. He had never again even seen the tall, pale man in a bathrobe who had come to his door to complain. Once, when he went to the toilet, the door had not opened when he turned the handle and a voice from inside had called, "It's occupied!" It had seemed to him that it was the tall, pale man's voice, but since he had not waited—because he didn't want to embarrass the man when he came out or make him self-conscious about the rustle of the toilet paper—he was never sure.

5

The Mysteries

Four nights in succession, the neighbours knocked on the walls.

Whenever Trelkovsky's friends saw him now they immediately began making fun of him. And when his colleagues in the office learned of the situation they joined in the general hilarity over his panicky conduct.

"You're wrong to let them intimidate you this way," Scope kept telling him. "If you let them get away with it, they'll never stop. Believe me—just act as if they didn't exist, and they'll soon get tired of bothering you."

But in spite of all his efforts, Trelkovsky was incapable of "acting as if they didn't exist".

Never at any moment when he was in the apartment could he rid himself of the thought that there was someone up above, someone down below, and others next door. But even if he had succeeded in forgetting them, they would have made a point of reminding him of their presence. Not that they made any undue amount of noise, of course; no, it wasn't that, it was just a succession of discreet rustling sounds, of almost imperceptible creakings, of muffled coughing, of doors grating softly on their hinges.

Occasionally, someone knocked. Trelkovsky went to open the door, but there was no one there. He went out on the landing and leaned over the rail. Then he might glimpse a door closing on the floor beneath, or hear an unsteady footstep begin to descend the stairs from the floor above. But it was never anything that directly concerned him.

At night, the sound of snoring would jerk him suddenly awake. But there was never anyone else in his bed. The sound came from somewhere else; it was one of the neighbours who was snoring. Trelkovsky would lie awake for hours, motionless and silent in the darkness, listening to the sleeping noises of the anonymous neighbour. He tried to call up a mental picture of what sort of person it might be. A man or a woman, with a mouth opened wide, the sheet pulled up so that it covered the bottom half of the face, or perhaps thrown back, leaving the shoulders and chest uncovered. One hand hanging over the side of the bed, perhaps. He would fall asleep again at last, but a few minutes later he would be awakened again by the ringing of an alarm clock. Then, somewhere else, a fumbling hand would restore silence by pressing a little button. Trelkovsky's fumbling hand, automatically searching for a little button of his own, served no purpose at all.

"You'll see," Scope said, "you'll get used to it in time. You had neighbours in the place where you used to live, but you didn't worry about them like this."

"If you stop making any noise," Simon added, "they'll think they've won. And then they'll never let you alone. Suzanne told me that when they first moved into their apartment the neighbours tried to make trouble for her because of the baby. So her husband bought a set of drums, and whenever anyone said anything to her about the baby he got out the drums and played for hours. No one bothers them any more."

Trelkovsky genuinely admired the courage of Suzanne's husband. He thought that he must be a big man, and strong. He would have to be to act the way he did. Unless, on the contrary, he was small and puny, but determined not to let himself be pushed around just because of his size. But in that case, the thing that puzzled Trelkovsky was why the neighbours hadn't simply beaten him up. Of course, if he were big and strong, they wouldn't dare try. But if he were small and puny? Perhaps they had just decided it wasn't important—and in fact, it wasn't. The problem was whether all neighbours would feel the same way. In his own case—what would happen with his neighbours if he were to behave in the same way? He suddenly remembered a clause in the lease which forbade him from playing a musical instrument.

Whenever he did anything in the office like dropping a penholder or something of the sort, his colleagues would pound on the wall with their fists and call out, "You're not going to let us sleep again?" or, "How long are you going to keep up this racket?" They laughed like children when they saw the terrified expression on Trelkovsky's face. He knew that it was just a joke, that this wasn't real, but even though he tried to be calm his heart always began thumping against his ribs. He smiled, as if it were all very amusing, but he was miserable.

One night, Scope invited him to his apartment.

"You'll see," he said. "I don't worry about these things."

He turned on the record player as soon as they entered, and set it at its maximum volume. In mortal terror, Trelkovsky listened to the rumbling of the brasses and the explosion of the percussion instruments. He had the impression that he was sitting in the very centre of the orchestra. And everyone else must have had the same impression, especially the neighbours. Trelkovsky felt himself going scarlet with embarrassment. There was only one thing in the world he wanted at that moment; to turn the dial and restore peace and quiet to the room.

Scope laughed maliciously. "What's the matter?" he asked. "Are you shocked? No, leave it alone—you'll see; I know what I'm doing."

Trelkovsky was forced to call on every ounce of will-power he had just to remain in his chair. What a way to act! What must the neighbours think? It seemed to him that the music was nothing but an enormous, unseemly belching. An infernally noisy display from an organism that should have been silent.

Finally, he couldn't stand it any longer. "Turn it down a little," he suggested timidly.

"No, leave it alone," Scope shouted, above the din. "Why should you worry about it? I told you I knew what I was doing." Then he added, laughing, "They're used to it by now."

Trelkovsky put his hands to his ears. "But it's too loud, even for us."

"You're not used to it, eh? Then why don't you enjoy it while you can—you can't do it at home!"

At that moment, someone knocked at the door. Trelkovsky jumped.

"A neighbour?" he demanded anxiously.

"I hope so. You'll see how these things should be handled."

And of course it was a neighbour.

"I'm sorry to bother you, monsieur," he began. "I see you have company ... I wonder if you could turn down the sound a little; my wife is ill ..."

Scope's face turned an angry, mottled purple. "So!" he shouted, "she's sick, is she? Well what do you think I'm going to do about it—stop living, just because of her? If she's sick, why doesn't she go to the hospital? You can keep your sob stories for someone else, they don't mean anything to me! I'll play my records if I want to, and as loud as I want to! I'm deaf myself, but I don't intend to be deprived of listening to music just because of that!"

He pushed the neighbour back onto the landing and slammed the door in his face.

"And don't try to pull any tricks," he shouted at the door, "I know the superintendent of police!"

Then he turned back to Trelkovsky, smiling broadly. "You see? That's the way to get rid of them."

Trelkovsky said nothing. He was incapable of speech. An attempt to pronounce so much as a word would have choked him. He could not watch a human being humiliated in this manner. He could still see the expression on the neighbour's face as he recoiled from Scope's angry shouting. The depths of his confusion had been reflected in his eyes. What could he say to his wife when he went back to his own apartment? Would he try to pretend that it was he who had done the shouting, or would he admit his ignominious defeat?

Trelkovsky was overcome. "But if his wife is sick ..." he murmured.

"So what? I don't give a —— for his wife. I don't go looking for him to tell him to be quiet when I'm sick. And he won't come back here, either—I'll guarantee you that."

Fortunately, Trelkovsky met no one on the staircase when he left. He made himself a promise that he would never go to visit Scope at home again.

"If you could have seen Trelkovsky's face when I told

that fellow off," Scope told Simon. "He looked as if he didn't know where to hide!"

They burst out laughing. Trelkovsky loathed both of them.

"He may be right, at that," Simon said. "Look at this." He took a newspaper from his coat pocket and unfolded it. "How's this for a headline? DRUNK, HE SANG 'TOSCA' AT THREE O'CLOCK IN THE MORNING, HIS NEIGHBOUR SHOOTS HIM WITH REVOLVER. Interesting, don't you think?"

Trelkovsky and Scope tried to snatch the newspaper from his hands, but Simon brushed them off. "Don't be so impatient," he said. "I'll read it to you. 'Last night was an active one for tenants of the building located at No. 8, Avenue Gambetta, in Lyon. For one of them, indeed, it was fatal. Monsieur Louis D—, forty-seven years old, bachelor, salesman for a manufacturing concern, had celebrated the successful negotiation of a contract with some friends, and had drunk more than was good for him. When he returned home, at about three o'clock in the morning, he decided to entertain his neighbours with a few operatic arias, since he was very proud of his singing voice. After several long excerpts from *Faust*, he had begun on *Tosca* when one of his neighbours, Monsieur Julien P—, fifty years old, married, wine broker, directed him to stop. Monsieur D— refused, and as an indication of his determination to go on with the concert went out to the landing, to sing from there. Monsieur P— then returned to his apartment and brought out an automatic pistol, which he emptied into the unfortunate drunkard. Monsieur D— was taken immediately to a hospital, where he died shortly after arrival. The murderer has been arrested.' "

While Simon was reading and Scope laughing loudly, Trelkovsky had felt an emotional knot forming in his throat. He had to clench his teeth tightly together to keep from crying. The same thing had happened to him often before, for the most absurd reasons, and he was invariably more embarrassed by it than anyone else. An irresistible desire to break down in tears swept over him, forcing him to blow his nose repeatedly, in spite of the fact that he had no sign of a cold.

He bought a copy of the newspaper, so that he would have the article himself and could re-read it at home.

All through this period it had been impossible for him to see either Scope or Simon without being forced to listen to a flood of anecdotes about the conduct of neighbours. Even as they were telling him these stories they would demand news of the latest developments in his own situation. They were dying to be invited again to his apartment, in the hope of causing an irreparable scandal, which would bring the whole thing to a violent end. When Trelkovsky refused categorically to invite them, they threatened to come whether he asked them or not.

"You'll see," Simon announced, "we'll arrive at four o'clock in the morning and bang on the door and call you by name."

"Or," Scope intervened, "we might knock on the door on the floor beneath you, and ask for you."

"Or we might invite a few hundred people to a party at your place, and say it was supposed to be a surprise."

Trelkovsky's laughter was more miserable than ever. Scope and Simon were probably saying all this as a joke, but he couldn't be sure of that. He had the feeling that the mere sight of him now brought out the worst in them. Since they had scented a victim, they could very easily become killers.

"And the more they see of me, the more exciting the thing will become," he thought.

He was perfectly conscious of the absurdity of his behaviour, but he was incapable of changing it. This absurdity was an essential part of him. It was probably the most basic element of his personality.

That night, at home, he re-read the article in the newspaper.

"Even if I were drunk," he thought, "I would never be so inconsiderate as to sing arias from an opera at three o'clock in the morning."

He tried to imagine what would happen if, in spite of his best intentions ... But the thought was too much for him, and he burst out laughing, alone in his bed, doing his best to stifle the sound beneath the blankets.

From that point on, he avoided his friends. He had no desire to push them into some rash action, simply by his presence. If they lost sight of him, they might, perhaps, calm down. He almost never went out any more. He began to take pleasure in the evenings spent calmly at home, with no noise or commotion. This was sure to be proof of his good faith to the neighbours.

"If it should happen some time later on," he thought, "that there was noise in here, for some reason, they'll remember all the nights of absolute silence, and they'll have to forgive me."

He found, during the course of these evenings alone, that the building was a theatre for a series of strange phenomena which he spent many hours studying and observing. He tried in vain to understand them. He told himself repeatedly that he was probably attaching too much importance to trivial little facts that had no real significance. And yet, when he took down the refuse ...

The refuse normally accumulated in Trelkovsky's apartment for days and days. Since he almost always ate in restaurants, it consisted primarily of discarded papers and contained very little perishable matter. In spite of this, however, there were occasional chunks of bread brought home from the restaurant in his pockets, or the remains of a piece of cheese clinging to its pasteboard container. There was one evening when Trelkovsky could not put it off any longer. He gathered all of the waste together, dumped it into his blue refuse pail, and carried it down to the big dustbins in the courtyard. The refuse pail was filled to overflowing, and as he went down the steps bits of paper and cotton, fragments of orange peel, and various other items dropped behind him. Trelkovsky was too intent on his primary burden to gather them up.

"I'll take care of them on the way back," he told himself.

But when he came back, there was nothing there. Someone had cleaned it all away. Who? Who had been watching him, waiting until he was outside the door, and then gathered up the things he had dropped?

The neighbours?

But wouldn't their interest have been in pouncing on him immediately, insulting him, and threatening him with dire reprisals for having littered the staircase? The neighbours would certainly never have let pass such a splendid opportunity to demonstrate their hold on him.

No, it was someone else ... or some*thing* else.

It occurred to Trelkovsky that it might have been rats. Enormous rats creeping out of the cellar or the sewers, in search of food. The resulting sounds he had often heard from the staircase supported this hypothesis. But if it was rats, why didn't they attack the dustbins in the courtyard? And why, for that matter, had he never seen a single one of them?

The mystery of it frightened him. He put off taking down the refuse even longer than he had in the past, and when at last he forced himself to do it he was so nervous he dropped something on almost every step. But when he returned, all trace of this clearly marked trail had disappeared.

This was not, however, the only reason for Trelkovsky's aversion to the simple housekeeping chore of taking down the refuse. There was also the fact that it aroused in him an overpowering sense of shame.

When he lifted the cover of one of the dustbins, before emptying the contents of his own pail into it, he was always astonished by its neatness and order. His own refuse was the most indecent collection in the entire building. Repugnant and despicable. There was no resemblance between it and the honest, day-to-day, refuse of the other tenants. That had a solid, respectable appearance, and his did not. Trelkovsky was convinced that when the concierge inspected the dustbins the next morning she would know immediately what portion of their contents belonged to him. He could almost see the expression of disgust on her face when she thought of him. She would imagine him in some degrading posture, and her nostrils would wrinkle distastefully, as if they scented his own body smells in the refuse. In an attempt to make it more difficult for her to identify him, he sometimes went to the extent of reaching into the bin and mixing his refuse in with the others. But even as he did it he knew that the ruse was doomed to failure, since she would surely know that he was the only person who would have any interest in such a ridiculous scheme.

In addition to the puzzle of the disappearing refuse, there was another mystery in the building that fascinated Trelkovsky. It concerned the toilets. From his window—as the concierge had told him that first day—he could see everything that took place in the little room across the courtyard. At first, he had struggled valiantly against the temptation to watch, but the mere fact that the observation post was there had eventually broken down his resistance. After that, he fell into the habit of sitting before the window for hours on end, with all the lights in the apartment turned out, so that he might see without being seen.

He became an ardent spectator at the continuing parade of his neighbours. He saw them all, men and women, lower their trousers or lift their skirts, totally unselfconsciously, squat down, and then, after the inevitable gestures of necessary hygiene, button or zip up their clothing and pull the flush chain. He was too far away to hear the resultant rushing of water.

All of this was normal. What was not normal was the strange behaviour of some of the people who entered the room. They did not squat down, almost out of his sight, they did not adjust their clothing in any way; they did nothing at all. Trelkovsky would watch them closely, for several minutes at a stretch sometimes, and could never discern the slightest trace of movement. It was both absurd and disturbing. Even to have seen them indulge in some obscene or indecent activity would have been a source of relief to him. But no, there was nothing.

They would simply remain standing, absolutely motionless, for a period of time that varied from one occasion to the next, and then, as if they were obeying some invisible signal, they would pull the chain and leave. There were women as well as men, but Trelkovsky was never able to make out their features. What reasons could they possibly have for behaving like this? The need for a period of solitude? Vice? An obligation to conform to some peculiar ritual, if by chance they all belonged to a sect of which he knew nothing? How could he find out?

He bought a second-hand pair of opera glasses, but they taught him nothing. The individuals whose conduct intrigued him so were really doing nothing at all, and their faces were unknown to him. Moreover, they were never the same, and he never saw any one of them a second time.

Once, when one of these individuals was engaged in his incomprehensible task, Trelkovsky resolved to set his mind at rest once and for all, and raced across to the toilet. He arrived too late; there was no one there. He sniffed the air, but there was no smell, and the toilet seat showed no sign of having been used.

Several times after that he tried to take one of these mysterious visitors by surprise, but he always arrived after they had left. One night, he thought he had at last succeeded. The door would not open; it was held fast by the little steel bolt which guaranteed the occupant's privacy. Trelkovsky waited patiently, determined not to leave before he had learned who that occupant was.

He did not have to wait very long. Monsieur Zy came out, nonchalantly buttoning his trousers. Trelkovsky smiled at him amiably, but Monsieur Zy ignored him completely. He walked off with his head held high, every inch a man who has no reason to be ashamed of his actions.

What was Monsieur Zy doing here? He must certainly have a toilet in his own apartment. Why, then, didn't he use that?

Trelkovsky gave up trying to solve these mysteries. But he went on studying them and forming conclusions which never completely satisfied him.

6

The Robbery

Someone had knocked again. This time it came from the apartment above. And he had not caused any great amount of noise. This is what had happened.

On that particular night, Trelkovsky had gone directly home from the office. He was not hungry, and since he was also a little short of money, he had decided to spend the evening getting his few belongings in order. Although he had been in the apartment for two months now, he had never unpacked anything beyond his daily necessities. As soon as he arrived, therefore, he opened the two suitcases, but then he forgot about them and began examining his surroundings with a critical eye. The eye of an engineer about to embark on some vast project of reclamation.

Since it was still early, he decided to move the big armoire from the wall against which it stood, but he was extremely careful to make as little noise as possible. He had never before attempted anything like this in the apartment. Until tonight, the arrangement of the furniture had seemed to him as unchangeable as the walls themselves.

He had, of course, moved the bed out into the front room on the unhappy night of the housewarming, but a bed wasn't really a piece of furniture.

Behind the armoire, he made a strange discovery. Beneath the fleecy layers of dust that covered the wall, there was a hole. Just a small excavation, really, about three feet above the floor, but he could see that a little greyish ball of cotton wool had been stuffed into it. Intrigued by this new mystery, he went to get a pencil, and used this to pry out the wad of cotton. There was something else behind it. He was forced to prod about for a minute or two with the pencil before the object finally rolled out into the palm of his left hand. It was a tooth. An incisor tooth, to be exact.

Why was he so suddenly overwhelmed by emotion when he remembered the yawning cavity of Simone Choule's mouth as she lay on her bed in the hospital? He could still see, with startling clarity, the empty space where an upper incisor should have been, a breach in the rampart of teeth, through which death had entered. Staring down at the tooth, and rolling it mechanically back and forth in his palm, he tried to imagine why Simone Choule would have put it in a hole in the wall.

He vaguely remembered some childhood legend in which a tooth hidden in this manner was mysteriously replaced by a gift for the child. Was it possible that the former tenant had still believed in such childish fantasies? Or had she just been unwilling—and Trelkovsky could have understood this perfectly—to part with something that was, after all, a part of herself? Trelkovsky recalled having read about a man who had lost an arm in a car accident and wanted to bury it in a cemetery. The authorities had refused permission and the arm had been incinerated, but the newspaper had not reported what happened after that.

Had they also refused to return the ashes of his arm to him? And if so, by what right?

Naturally, a tooth or an arm was no longer part of a person, once it had been removed. But it was not really as simple as all that.

"At what precise moment," Trelkovsky asked himself, "does an individual cease to be the person he—and everyone else—believes himself to be? I have to have an arm amputated, all right. I say: myself and my arm. If both of them are gone, I say: myself and my two arms. If it were my legs it would be the same thing: myself and my legs. If they had to take out my stomach, my liver, my kidneys—if that were possible—I could still say: myself and my organs. But if they cut off my head, what could I say then? Myself and my body, or myself and my head? By what right does the head, which isn't even a member like an arm or a leg, claim the title of 'myself'? Because it contains the brain? But there are larvae and worms, and probably all sorts of other things, that don't possess a brain. What about creatures like those? Are there brains that exist somewhere, and say: myself and my worms?"

Trelkovsky had been on the point of throwing the tooth away, but at the last minute he changed his mind. In the end, he just changed the ball of cotton wool for a new and cleaner one, and replaced it in the hole.

But now his curiosity had been aroused. He began exploring the room inch by inch, and he was soon rewarded. Underneath a small commode he found a package of letters and a pile of books, all of it black with dust. He found a rag and gave them a preliminary cleaning. The books were all historical novels, and the letters seemed of no importance, but Trelkovsky promised himself that he would read them later. In the meantime, he wrapped the whole bundle in yesterday's newspaper and climbed up on a chair to put them out of sight on the top of the armoire. It was then that the catastrophe occurred. The package slipped out of his hands and fell noisily to the floor.

The reaction of the neighbours was almost instantaneous. He had not yet stepped down from the chair when there was a series of furious thumpings on the ceiling. Was it already after ten o'clock at night? He looked at his watch: it was ten minutes after ten.

He threw himself down on the bed, literally consumed with rage, determined not to make a move for the rest of the night and thereby deprive them of the pleasure of any new pretext for intervention.

Someone knocked at the door.

It was the neighbours!

Trelkovsky cursed the panic that swept over him like a wave. He could hear the sound of his own heart, echoing the knocking at the door. He would have to do something. He stifled the flood of curses that rose unbidden in his mouth.

So he was going to have to justify himself again, to explain everything he did, to ask forgiveness for the mere fact that he was alive! He was going to have to be sufficiently weak-willed to rid himself of his hatred and remain indifferent to anything that was said. He was going to have to say something like: look at me, I'm not worthy of your anger, I'm nothing but a dumb animal who can't prevent the noisy symptoms of his decay, so don't waste your time with me, don't dirty your hands by hitting me, just try to put up with the fact that I exist. I'm not asking you to like me, I know that that's impossible, because I'm not likeable, but at least do me the kindness of despising me enough to ignore me.

Whoever it was at the door knocked again, and he went to open it.

59

He saw at once that it was not one of the neighbours. He wasn't arrogant enough, not sure enough of his own rights, there was too clear a light of uncertainty in his eyes. The sight of Trelkovsky seemed to surprise him.

"Isn't this Mademoiselle Choule's apartment?" he stammered.

Trelkovsky nodded vaguely. "Yes—that is, it used to be. I'm the new tenant."

"Oh. She's moved then?"

Trelkovsky didn't know what to say. Obviously the man knew nothing of Simone Choule's death. But what were his ties of friendship with her? Just friendship, or perhaps love? Could he just come right out and tell him about her suicide?

"Come in," he said at last. "I didn't mean to keep you standing out there like that."

The stranger murmured thanks, in a kind of confused mumble. He was clearly very upset.

"Nothing has happened to her, I hope," he said hesitantly.

Trelkovsky was almost equally distressed. What if he should start screaming, or something like that? The neighbours would never miss an opportunity like that. He coughed, trying to clear his throat.

"Please sit down, monsieur . . ."

"Badar, Georges Badar."

"I'm delighted to meet you, Monsieur Badar. My name is Trelkovsky. I'm afraid there has been an unfortunate . . ."

"My God, Simone!"

He had almost been shouting. "They say the greatest sorrows are silent," Trelkovsky thought. "I only hope it's true!"

"Did you know her well?" he asked.

The man leapt to his feet. "Did you say, *did* I know her? Is she—is she dead then?"

"She committed suicide," Trelkovsky murmured, "a little over two months ago."

"Simone . . . Simone . . ."

He was speaking very softly now. The thin line of his moustache was trembling, his lips clenched together convulsively, his Adam's apple slid up and down behind the starched collar of his shirt.

"She threw herself out of the window," Trelkovsky said. "If you would like to see . . ." Almost unconsciously, he was repeating the words of the concierge. "She hit a glass roof over the courtyard, on the first floor. She didn't die right away."

"But why? Why would she have done that?"

"No one seems to know. Do you know her friend Stella?" Badar shook his head. "She doesn't know either, and she was her closest friend. It's a terrible thing. Would you like a drink?"

He realized as soon as he had said it that there was nothing to drink in the apartment.

"Let's go down to the café," he suggested, "and I'll buy you a drink. It will do you good."

Two things had induced Trelkovsky to make this proposal, in spite of his impoverished condition. The first was the really disturbing state of mind of the young man, and his frightening pallor. The other was fear of an outburst that would attract the wrath of the neighbours.

In the café, he learned from Badar that he had been a childhood friend of Simone's, that he had always loved her secretly, and that he had just returned from his military service and decided to confess his love and ask her to marry him. Badar was a dull young man, and almost inconceivably trite. His distress was clearly sincere, but it was expressed in phrases he had borrowed from cheap novels. To his mind, the ready-made formulas he used doubtless constituted a more important tribute to the deceased than anything he might have thought of himself. He was curiously touching in his ignorance. After the second cognac, he began to talk of suicide.

"I want to be with the woman I love," he stammered, with tears in his voice. "Life isn't worth living any more."

"You mustn't think that way," Trelkovsky said, adopting Badar's cliché-ridden form of speech. "You're young; you'll forget . . ."

"Never," Badar answered, staring into his glass as though it contained a lethal dose of poison.

"There are lots of other women in the world," Trelkovsky announced. "They may not take her place, but at least they can help to fill the void in your heart. You should go away, do anything at all, but force yourself to keep busy, to meet other people. You'll see—you'll be all right then."

"Never!" Badar repeated, and swallowed the last of his cognac.

After this café they went to another, and then to still another. The man was desperate, and Trelkovsky did not dare leave him alone. So they wandered from one bar to the next all night long, while Trelkovsky supplied the proper dogmatic responses to the long litany of Badar's despair. And finally, as the sun was coming up, he secured a postponement of the projected suicide. Badar reluctantly agreed to go on living for at least another month before making any final decision.

As he walked back home alone, Trelkovsky began to sing. He was exhausted, and slightly drunk, but in excellent humour. The almost ritual phrasing of the conversation had delighted him. It had all been so deliciously artificial! It was only reality that found him unprepared and defenceless.

The doors to the café across the street from his apartment were just being opened when he arrived. Trelkovsky went in to have some breakfast.

"Do you live across the street?" the waiter asked him.

Trelkovsky nodded. "Yes. But I haven't been there very long."

"You're in the apartment of the girl who committed suicide?"

"Yes. Did you know her?"

"I certainly did. She came in here every morning. I never even waited for her to order—I just brought her her chocolate and dry toast. She didn't drink coffee, because it made her too nervous. She told me once that if she drank coffee in the morning she couldn't sleep for two days."

"That's true," Trelkovsky agreed. "It does make you nervous. But I'm too used to it now; I couldn't get along without my morning coffee."

"You can say that because there's nothing wrong with you now," the waiter said smugly, "but the day something happens and you get sick, you'll stop drinking it."

"Perhaps," Trelkovsky said.

"No doubt about it. Of course there are some people who can't drink chocolate, on account of their liver, but she wasn't one of those. There can't have been anything wrong with her in that way."

"No, I guess not," Trelkovsky said.

"It's too bad, though. A woman like that, who's still young, and kills herself, and nobody knows why. And probably for nothing at all. A fit of depression, the feeling you've had it and—hop!—you give up. Shall I bring you a chocolate?"

Trelkovsky did not answer. He was thinking about the

63

former tenant again. He drank the chocolate without realizing that it wasn't coffee, paid his bill and left. When he reached the third floor landing he noticed that the door to his apartment was standing slightly open. His eyebrows came together in a puzzled frown.

"That's odd," he thought. "I was certain I closed it."

He pushed the door open and went inside. The greyish light of early morning filtered wanly through the curtains at the solitary window.

He was not worried, but greatly surprised. He thought of the neighbours first, then of Monsieur Zy, and then of Simon and Scope. Was it possible that they had actually carried out one of their idiotic plans? He pulled back the curtains and surveyed the room around him. The door to the armoire was wide open, and its contents were strewn across the bed. Someone had searched through everything he owned.

The first thing he knew to be missing was the radio. And shortly after that he realized that his two suitcases were gone.

He no longer had a past.

Not that there was anything very valuable in the suitcases—just an inexpensive camera, a pair of shoes, and some books. But there were also some snapshots of himself as a child, as well as some of his parents and the girls he had loved when he was still an adolescent, a few letters, a collection of souvenirs of the farthest reaches of his memory. Tears flooded his eyes when he thought of them.

He took off one of his shoes and hurled it across the room. The angry gesture relieved him.

Someone rapped on the wall.

"All right!" he shouted. "I know I'm making too much noise! But you should have rapped while this was going on, not now!"

He made an effort to control himself. "It's not their fault, after all. And besides, perhaps they did rap while it was going on."

What should he do? Make a complaint? Yes, that was it; he would go and make a complaint at the police station. He looked at his watch: it was seven o'clock. Would the police station be open now? The best thing to do was to go and see. He put on his shoe again and started down the staircase. He met Monsieur Zy on the ground floor landing.

"You've disturbed everyone again, Monsieur Trelkovsky," the landlord said angrily. "This can't go on any longer. All of the neighbours are complaining."

"I beg your pardon, Monsieur Zy," Trelkovsky said, "but are you talking about last night?"

His self-assurance took Monsieur Zy by surprise. He could not understand why his anger seemed to have no effect on his tenant, and consequently he was annoyed.

"Of course I'm talking about last night," he said. "You made a fiendish racket, again. I thought I had managed to make you realize that you wouldn't stay in my house much longer if you went on acting that way. But I see that I'm going to be forced to take other measures . . ."

"I have been robbed, Monsieur Zy," Trelkovsky interrupted. "I just came in a few minutes ago, and I found the door to my apartment open. I was on my way to the police station now, to register a complaint."

The landlord's expression changed completely. His air of stern remonstrance vanished, to be replaced by a look that was positively threatening.

"What do you mean?" he shouted. "My house is a respectable place. If you're trying to get out of this by inventing some kind of story . . ."

"But it's true!" Trelkovsky was shouting too. "Don't

65

you understand what I'm saying? My apartment was broken into. I've been robbed!"

Monsieur Zy did not answer immediately, and then he said calmly, "I understand you perfectly. And I'm very sorry. But why are you going to the police station?"

It was Trelkovsky who was taken by surprise this time. "Why—to tell them what happened," he stammered. "To tell them what was stolen, so they'll know which things are mine if they catch the thieves."

Monsieur Zy's expression had undergone still another transformation. He was benevolent, almost paternal, now.

"Now look, Monsieur Trelkovsky," he said, "this is an honest house. My tenants are honest people . . ."

"It's not a question of that . . ." Trelkovsky began.

"Let me finish. You know how people are. If they see policemen here, God knows what they'll think and say. You know how careful I am about selecting my tenants. In your own case—I let you have the apartment because I was convinced you were an honest man. If I hadn't been, you could have offered me ten million francs and I would have laughed in your face. If you go to the police now, they'll send men here and ask all kinds of questions— useless questions, of course, but they can have a disastrous effect on the opinion of the other tenants. And I'm not saying that just for my own sake, but for yours too."

"For mine! But what have I done?" Trelkovsky could not contain his astonishment.

"I know it may seem crazy to you," the landlord said soothingly, "but people who get involved with the police are always regarded with suspicion. I know that, in this case, you are perfectly within your rights, but other people won't know that. They'll suspect you of God knows what, and me, too, for that matter. No; believe me, I know what I'm saying. I know the superintendent of police, and

I'll talk to him about this. He'll know what should be done. In that way, no one can reproach you for not having done your duty as a citizen and we'll avoid all the neighbourhood gossip."

Trelkovsky was too stunned to object.

"Oh, and by the way," Monsieur Zy added, "the former tenant always wore slippers after ten o'clock. It was much more comfortable for her—and much more pleasant for the people below her!"

PART TWO
———
THE NEIGHBOURS

7

The Battle

There was a battle going on, right in the heart of the building. Trelkovsky was hidden behind his curtains, watching the spectacle in the courtyard and laughing delightedly. As soon as the first sounds of argument reached his ears he had hurriedly extinguished all the lights, so that he could not be wrongly accused of anything when it was all over.

It had started in the building across the way, where the fourth floor was celebrating an anniversary of some kind. The rooms were so brightly lit that they constituted a challenge in themselves. The windows were tightly closed, because of the cold, but even so the sound of laughter and singing could be clearly heard. Trelkovsky had foreseen from the very first that the festivities would take a tragic turn. And in his own mind he had been fervently grateful to the troublemakers. "They're just as bad as any of the others," he thought. "I've already heard them complaining about the noise from the fifth floor, but that's not important. It'll be a case of the wolves devouring each other!"

The first reaction had been a plaintive, but nonetheless

THE TENANT

shrill voice, asking for silence for the sake of a sick woman.
There was no answer to that. The second attempt, much
more direct, was a shouted, "Why don't you shut up down
there? We have to work tomorrow!" Again, there was no
reply. Just more laughter and singing. Trelkovsky revelled
in the possibilities of this noisy pleasure. A silence that
was heavy with menace had settled over every other corner
of the building. One by one, the lights had gone out,
demonstrating to all the world that the tenants within
wanted to sleep. It was with the assurance of being well
within their rights that two masculine voices then bluntly
demanded silence again. A brisk dialogue ensued.

"Can't a person even celebrate an anniversary any
more?"

"All right, but enough is enough. Nobody minded your
celebrating up to a decent hour, but now it's time to call it
off. Other people have to work tomorrow!"

"We have to work tomorrow too, but we have a right
to a little fun now and then, don't we?"

"Look, you've been told to call it off, to stop the noise.
What do we have to do to convince you?"

"If you think you're scaring me, you're barking up the
wrong tree! I don't like people giving me orders—we'll do
as we damned well please!"

"Oh, you will, eh? Well why don't you just come downstairs for a minute, and we'll see about that?"

"Oh, shut up!"

Having arrived at this stage, the voices from either side
of the courtyard began showering insults on each other,
descending at last to a level of vulgarity that made Trelkovsky blush. All the guests on the fourth floor joined in
a resounding chorus of song, to prove their solidarity with
their host. This development produced immediate reaction
from windows which had been silent until now. An

avalanche of oaths and imprecations descended on the revellers. Then the two masculine voices that had opened the battle engaged in a brief colloquy of their own, and decided to go down to the courtyard and settle this thing with the enemy once and for all.

The enemy required a little urging, but Trelkovsky was sure they wouldn't hold out for very long. He could already hear the shouting from the court beneath his window.

"You go that way, and I'll take this part. Call me if you catch one of them. Why don't you come down, you bastards?"

"I saw something over there—just wait till I get my hands on you, you ——!"

Trelkovsky was no longer laughing. He was beginning to be frightened. He could see that the mutual hatred of these men was no pretence. They were not playing. They seemed to have instinctively rediscovered their wartime reflexes, to have suddenly remembered things they had been taught in the army. They were no longer peaceful tenants, but killers in search of a victim. With his face pressed hard against the window pane, he followed the developments of the conflict. After a complete circuit of the courtyard, the two masculine voices had now rejoined each other at its centre.

"You didn't see anything?"

"No, I caught up with someone in the hall, but he said he wasn't one of them so I let him go."

"They're afraid to come down, the bastards! But they'll have to go home sometime, and then . . ."

There was a sudden clattering sound, as the windows on the fourth floor were thrown violently open.

"All right, you asked for it! Just stay right where you are, and we'll see who's giving the orders around here!"

In spite of the distance, Trelkovsky could hear the sound of footsteps pounding heavily down the stairs. In the courtyard below, the two masculine voices were jubilant.

"They took their time about it, but they're coming! We'll show them, the bastards—teach them to tear the place apart in the middle of the night . . ."

The encounter must have taken place beneath the shattered glass roof, somewhere near the dustbins, because Trelkovsky heard several of them overturn noisily, punctuating the stream of cursing and shouts of rage. Then someone began to run, trying to reach the relative safety of the staircase. A silhouette detached itself from the general mêlée and hurled itself savagely at the fleeing man. The two figures rolled across the ground, punching and kicking at each other with spectacular agility, but never letting go. One of them finally secured his position on top, seized his opponent's head by the ears, and began pounding it methodically against the concrete path.

The sirens of a police car abruptly drowned out the piercing cries of the women who were now clustered at the windows, and uniformed policemen invaded the courtyard. Within a split second there was no one else in sight. Then the sirens wailed off into the night, and calm returned.

That night, Trelkovsky dreamed that he got out of his bed, pulled it away from the wall, and discovered a door in the area concealed behind the headboard. Astonished by this unexpected find, he opened the door and found himself in a long corridor. An underground passage, really, sloping downward into the ground, growing steadily larger as he moved along it, and ending finally in an enormous, empty room with neither doors nor windows. Its walls were totally bare. He walked back through the underground passage, and when he came to the door behind the bed he saw that there was a shiny new lock on the side of it facing into the passage. When he slid the bolt back and forth it functioned smoothly and silently. He was suddenly possessed by a creeping sense of terror, wondering what sort of creature could have put this lock in place, where he had come from, where he had gone, and why, tonight, he had left the bolt open.

Someone was knocking on the door. Trelkovsky awoke with a start.

"Who's there?" he called.

"It's me," a woman's voice answered.

He put on an old bathrobe and went to open.

A woman he had never seen before was standing on the threshold, clutching the hand of a girl of about twenty. From the expression in the girl's eyes, Trelkovsky recognized at once that she was a mute.

"What can I do for you?" he asked.

The woman must have been about sixty, perhaps a trifle older. Her eyes were very black, and she was staring directly into Trelkovsky's face. She made a little gesture with the sheet of paper she held in her free hand.

"Was it you, monsieur, who registered a complaint about me?"

"A complaint?"

"Yes—for causing a disturbance at night."

Trelkovsky was dumbfounded. "I've never made any kind of complaint!" he said angrily.

The woman promptly burst into tears. She seemed to collapse against the slight figure of the girl, who was observing Trelkovsky intently.

"Someone made a complaint about me," the woman said. "I got this paper this morning. But it isn't me—she's the one who makes all the noise. All night long."

75

"Who do you mean—she?" Trelkovsky asked, more bewildered than ever.

"That old woman. She's a nasty old woman, monsieur. She does everything she can to make things hard for me. Just because I have a crippled daughter ..." She lifted the long skirt that shrouded the girl's legs, and pointed to the heavy orthopaedic shoe on her left foot. "She hates me, because I have a crippled daughter. And now I get a letter saying that I make disturbances at night! It's not you, monsieur? You're not the one who made the complaint?"

"Of course not," Trelkovsky said. "I told you, I've never made a complaint."

"Then it must be her. I asked downstairs, but they hadn't done it either. They said it might have been you. But it must be that old woman." Her face was bathed in tears, her voice cracked and faltering. "I don't make any noise, monsieur. I go to bed very early, every night. I'm not like her. If I were, I would have made a complaint about her, long before this. She's an old woman, monsieur, and like all old women she can't get to sleep at night, so she walks up and down in her apartment, she moves furniture, and she keeps me from sleeping—and my daughter, too. I had the most awful time finding this hovel we live in, monsieur; I sold all of my jewellery, I sweated blood, and if that old woman has me thrown out I don't know where we'll go. Do you know what she did, monsieur?"

Trelkovsky shook his head, but the woman had obviously not expected an answer, because she went ahead with her story almost without a pause.

"She put a broom across my door, to keep me from going out. She wedged it against the doorknob—you could see it was done deliberately—and when I tried to go out that morning I couldn't open the door. I pulled and pulled and I must have twisted something in my shoulder. It was black and blue for days. And do you know what she told me? She said she had just left it there by accident! And now she's made a complaint about me; I have to go to the police station. If she has me thrown out . . ."

"But she can't have you thrown out," Trelkovsky said, feeling an enormous sympathy for the unhappy woman. "She can't do anything like that."

"Do you really think so? I never make any noise, monsieur, honestly . . ."

"Even if you did, she couldn't do anything! They don't have the right to throw you out if you have nowhere else to go. She couldn't do it . . ."

The woman seemed slightly reassured. She thanked Trelkovsky, between little fits of sobbing, and started down the staircase, still leaning on her daughter.

Where did she live? Trelkovsky leaned across the railing, trying to see where she went, but she did not stop on the floor below. She disappeared from sight before he could learn anything.

He went back into his own apartment, and as he shaved and dressed to go to the office he kept turning over in his mind this business of the complaint. When he considered it objectively, it looked very suspicious. In the first place, he didn't even know where this woman lived; and in the second, he thought it odd that the tenants beneath him— the landlord and his wife—would have given his name as the probable plaintiff. Wasn't it much more likely that they had wanted to show him what could happen to him if he continued to disturb the neighbours? Without meaning to say anything wrong about her, wasn't it possible that this woman had been paid to come to his door and play this part? Who was the old woman she kept talking about? He had never seen anyone in the building who remotely resembled her description. Something about the whole story rang very false.

He went down the stairs as silently as possible. He had no desire to meet Monsieur Zy this morning. He was forced, as always, to make a mock genuflection in front of the row of post boxes in the courtyard, to see if there was anything in his. There were two letters.

One was addressed to Mademoiselle Choule, and the other to himself. It was not the first time he had received mail intended for the former tenant. At first, he had hesitated about opening it, but his curiosity had gradually overcome this initial repugnance; he had told himself that he really should see if it was anything important, and from then on he had opened everything. His own letter was of no importance—a mimeographed advertisement. He crumpled it into a ball and threw it in the dustbin as he passed. He went to the café across the street for his morning coffee. The waiter greeted him cheerfully.

"Coffee? No nerves today? What about chocolate?"

"Yes," Trelkovsky said. "Chocolate. And dry toast——two." He called the waiter back before he had had time to fill the order. "And bring me a packet of Gauloises."

The waiter spread his hands in a gesture of utter despair. "I'm out of them at the moment. I'll have to get some for you down the street."

Trelkovsky shrugged. "What do you have?"

"Gitanes—the straight Virginias. Mademoiselle Choule always used to smoke those. Shall I bring you a packet?"

"All right, Gitanes. But without a filter."

"Right. She didn't like the filtered ones either."

Trelkovsky had ripped open the flap of the letter addressed to Simone Choule. He read:

"Mademoiselle—I hope you will forgive the liberty I am taking in writing to you. A mutual friend, Pierre Aram, gave me your address, and told me that you might be able to give me some information which is extremely important to me. I live in Lyon, and work there as a sales clerk in a book shop. But personal reasons make it necessary for me to leave here and come to live in Paris. I have been offered a job in a book shop located at 80, rue de la Victoire. I must give the owners my reply within a week, but I am very uncertain about it at the moment, because I have just received an offer of another job in a shop located at 12, rue de Vaugirard. I don't know Paris very well, and I know nothing of these two shops. Since I will be getting a commission on sales, I should naturally like to learn a little more about the possibilities in each of them.

"Piere said he was sure that you would be kind enough to go and look at these two shops and send me your estimate of the choice I should make.

"I realize very clearly the inconvenience this may cause you, but I would be extremely grateful if you could do it for me, and let me know what you think, as quickly as possible. I am enclosing a stamped, self-addressed envelope. Thanking you in advance for this great kindness, etc. . . . etc. . . ."

The letter was signed with a full name and address—a woman, or even more likely, a young girl. There was also the stamped envelope she had mentioned.

"I'll have to answer it," Trelkovsky murmured. "That won't be any trouble."

8

Stella

Trelkovsky was leaving a cinema where he had seen a film about Louis XI. Ever since he had begun reading the historical novels left in the apartment by Simone Choule he was fascinated by everything having to do with history. On the street outside the cinema, he saw Stella.

She was surrounded by a group of friends; three young men and a girl. They had unquestionably come out of the same cinema. He hesitated to speak to her, but at the same time he felt a genuine need to do so; not so much because he wanted to see her again as to find himself in the company of people he did not know. Since he had been avoiding Scope and Simon he had lived almost entirely alone, and he was tormented by the desire to see and talk with others of his own kind.

He moved a trifle closer to the group, waiting for the moment when he might approach Stella. Unfortunately, she was standing with her back to him. From what little he could hear of the conversation, he gathered that she was talking about the film, and expressing her point of view with considerable vehemence. He waited patiently for a lull that would make it possible for him to break in. The group had been standing in front of the cinema at first, but now they had begun to walk slowly down the street, and Trelkovsky was forced to follow them. He felt for all the world like someone listening at a keyhole. No one had noticed him as yet, but they surely would in a moment or two. He had to do something, and promply, before one of her friends realized that he was following them and jumped to some nasty conclusion. But what should he do? If he simply called out, "Stella," wouldn't she think him too familiar? And what would her friends think? He knew that some people detested being called by name in a public place—she might be one of those. He couldn't just say, "Hey!" or "Hello, there!"—that was entirely too unceremonious. He thought about, "I beg your pardon," but that didn't seem much better. Snap his fingers, or gesture with his arms? Impolite—it was all right for calling a waiter in a café, but after all . . . He decided to cough.

She didn't hear him, of course. And then, quite suddenly, he knew what he should say:

"I hope I'm not interrupting . . ."

She seemed genuinely pleased to see him.

"Why no, not at all."

She introduced him to her friends, very vaguely, and made a point of remarking to Trelkovsky that they were also friends of Simone Choule. At first, he didn't know who she was talking about, but when he remembered he hastily assumed an expression of deep sorrow.

"Unfortunately, I didn't know her very well," he sighed.

Someone suggested that they go and have a drink in a nearby brasserie, and everyone agreed. A few minutes later they were all seated around a large table covered with some sort of ox-blood red plastic. Trelkovsky was seated next to Stella, and as she settled herself on the banquette he felt her thigh brush firmly against his trouser leg. He was tempted to look away, but forced himself to turn back to her. She smiled at him.

He thought her smile was almost obscene. All of her little affectations, in fact, seemed filled with sensual undertones. She apparently thought of nothing but making love. The manner in which she flicked the point of her tongue into the foam on her glass of beer was significant in itself. A drop of the beer escaped her lips and rolled slowly down the length of her chin and onto her neck. She lifted her hand lazily and blotted it out just as it reached the depression above her collarbone. For an instant, the mark of her finger remained white in the flesh, and then the blood flowed back and it was again a delicate pink.

It occurred to Trelkovsky, absurdly, that her flesh must still bear the traces of hundreds of fingerprints. As she leaned forward to replace her glass on the table, her coat slipped down on the seat behind her. She rid herself of it entirely by straightening up and throwing back her shoulders, causing her breasts to wiggle provocatively. Viewed from the side, where Trelkovsky sat, the contour of her bust stretched the material of her dress into a series of taut little folds just beneath the armpit. She seemed to be aware of it, because she reached across and tugged at it slightly, attempting to smooth it down. But the net result of this gesture was to reveal the outlines of her brassière, even to the rib-like lines that must be stays. Yes, he remembered now, her brassière did have stays.

And further down?

The skirt was tight around her hips, so that when she sat down it was pulled into dozens of horizontal folds, girdling her stomach and abdomen like silky ropes. The straps of her suspenders, and the suspenders themselves, were thrown into sharp relief. The skirt was so short it barely reached the rounded globes of her knees. She crossed her legs, and pulled the skirt down, then let her hand run the whole length of her leg, as though she were caressing it. Her fingernails produced a curious rustling sound as she drew them along the tinted nylon sheath. With the tip of her left foot, she was absent-mindedly massaging the calf of her right leg. She laughed.

"What do you say we all go over to my place?" one of the young men suggested.

She stood up and turned around to pick up her coat, bending down to straighten the rumpled sleeve on which she had been sitting. The upper part of her dress bloused out, and he could see the brassière, not quite retaining the fullness of the breasts. They trembled slightly as she lifted the coat. Their flesh was very white around the thin red line marking the area where the upper edge of the brassière normally pressed tight against them.

The waiter pocketed the coins they had put on the table and tore up the bill, signifying that now they had paid and were dismissed.

"Are you coming?" Stella asked.

He hesitated, but the fear of finding himself alone again swept away his doubts.

"If you want me to," he murmured.

The apartment was very close by. The young man to whom it belonged saw to it that they were all seated in the living-room, and then went to get ice and bottles from the refrigerator. The instant they crossed the threshold he had taken on all the mannerisms of the thoughtful host, the lord of the manor offering hospitality to a group of weary pilgrims. He put a record on the player, distributed glasses to everyone, and set out a tray containing the various bottles, a bucket of ice, and a bowl of little salted nuts. If anyone so much as looked at him he would leap to his feet and say, "Is something wrong? What can I get for you?" He was so obliging he was positively irritating. They all began talking at once.

"Do you know where I saw Simone the last time? It was at a concert—the Lamoureux—I bumped into her completely by chance. We talked for a while and I asked her how things were going. She said everything was fine, but you could see that there was something wrong."

"I still have a book she loaned me. One of those historical novels of hers. I haven't even read it."

"She didn't like the styles this year at all. She said the Chanels were the only thing she could possibly wear—the others all looked terrible on her."

"She told me she wanted to buy the Beethoven Fourth in that new recording for the Symphony Club."

"It's odd the way she hated animals . . ."

"It wasn't really that she hated them; she was afraid of them."

"I remember, she couldn't stand American films."

"She had a good voice, you know, but she never really tried to develop it."

"She went some place on the Cote d'Azur for her holiday, but I never knew where."

"She was always afraid of getting fat."

"That's why she never ate anything."

Trelkovsky had not joined in the conversation, but was listening intently to every word, periodically taking a little sip from the glass in his hand. Everything that was said, every new morsel of information about Simone Choule, was a revelation to him. So she had not liked this—and she did like that! How odd! Imagine dying when you had such positive ideas about things! There was something totally inconsistent about it.

He leaned forward in his chair and began asking questions of the others, hoping to learn more details about the former tenant of his apartment. Then he made mental notes, comparing her taste in things with his own. When they coincided, he felt absurdly pleased. But this didn't happen very often. She detested jazz, for instance, and he liked it. She adored Colette, and he had never managed to read a page of any one of her books. He had no appreciation whatever of Beethoven, and especially not of the symphonies. The Cote d'Azur was a part of France that held no interest for him at all. But he went on tenaciously, trying to learn everything he could, feeling rewarded whenever he came across the slightest similarity of taste.

The young man who was their host asked one of the girls to dance. Then another one asked Stella. Trelkovsky poured himself a second drink. He was slightly drunk. The third young man, who was not dancing, attempted to strike up a conversation with him, but he answered only in monosyllables. After the first dance, Stella came and asked him if he wanted to dance with her. He accepted.

He danced very seldom, and was not very good at it, but the alcohol he had consumed inspired him now. They danced several slow numbers very slowly indeed, holding each other very tight. Trelkovsky had arrived at the point where he cared nothing about what the others thought. He heard her whispering in his ear, asking if he wanted her to come home with him. He shook his head violently. What would she think if she knew his address! She didn't say anything, but he knew that she was annoyed, so he put his head close to hers and whispered in her ear, "Can't we go to your place?" She smiled at him, apparently mollified. "Yes, of course," she murmured. She must have been pleased at the thought, because her hands pressed even more strongly against his shoulder. He didn't understand her.

Everything in her apartment bespoke her sex. There were reproductions of Marie Laurencin paintings on the walls, side by side with highly polished shells and illustrations clipped from women's magazines. The floor was covered with a rug of woven straw. Empty bottles of differing colours decorated a sideboard. There was only one room; the bed was set in an alcove in the wall.

She stretched out on it languidly, and he followed her example. He knew what was expected of him at such a moment. He began to unfasten her dress, but his fingers were awkward about it and she was forced to help him. Her face looked more vulgar than ever. She knew what was about to happen and she was unashamedly enjoying every minute of it. In spite of his natural desires, Trelkovsky could not succeed in working up any real sense of excitement. Perhaps because of the alcohol he had drunk, but also because, for some strange reason, this woman horrified him.

She was far more excited than he. She even undid his belt and pulled off his trousers. And then she removed his shorts. His own voice came to him, saying stupidly, "Well, there we are."

He grasped her breasts firmly in his hands, as if they provided a much-needed point of support, and laboriously straddled her body. He closed his eyes. He was very sleepy.

She trembled violently, uttered a strangled little cry, and bit him. The idea that she should go to so much trouble to create this illusion of passion amused him. Very methodically, he entered her, imagining, even as he did so, that she was really a famous film star. Then the film star faded from his thoughts and was replaced by a girl in the bakery where he had bought his bread when he lived in the little studio room. Stella's body arched up against his.

It seemed to him now that there were two women on

the bed beneath him, then, quite suddenly, three. He remembered an erotic photograph Scope had shown him once. It showed three masked women, naked except for long black stockings, and swarming over the figure of a very hairy man. Then he tried repeating the word "thigh" to himself. This had no particular effect, so he gave it up and recalled an episode in his childhood when he had first touched a young girl's breasts. And that in turn called to mind the other women with whom he had done what he was doing now. Stella let out a low, throaty murmuring.

The film he had seen earlier that night suddenly came back to him. There was a scene in it that showed an attempted rape. The hero's fiancée would have been the beautiful victim, but of course she escaped at the last moment. The following sequence showed Cardinal Balue's mistress in the cage in which the king imprisoned her. Louis XI was laughing ominously as he forced her to sing for him. Trelkovsky thought it would be wonderfully amusing if all the old maids kept beautiful girls in cages, instead of canaries. Stella moaned softly.

When it was all over, he retained enough presence of mind to kiss her very gently. He didn't want to do anything that might hurt her feelings. Then they both went to sleep.

Trelkovsky woke up very shortly afterwards. His forehead was bathed in sweat, and the bed was pitching back and forth beneath him. He knew the feeling very well, and experience had taught him that he must get to the bathroom as quickly as possible. Stella had turned out the light before going to sleep, so he fumbled in the darkness for the switch, trying to remember where it had been. He found it at last, and got up, staggering slightly. The door to the bathroom was just next to the kitchen. He knelt down in front of the bowl of the toilet seat, put his forearm across its rim and rested his forehead on his arm. His head was just above the circular well of the bowl and he could hear the continuous gurgling of the water. His stomach turned inside out, like a glove, and he vomited.

It wasn't disagreeable at all. Almost like a liberation, in fact. A kind of suicide, in a way. These particles of matter that showered from his mouth, after he had thought them consumed and digested, did not disgust him. No, he was completely indifferent to them; and to everything else, for that matter. It was only when he vomited that he could be indifferent even to life itself. He forced himself to make as little noise as possible, and experienced a curious sense of comfort in his awkward position.

He felt better now. He thought back to what had happened earlier and a little shiver ran through his body. He was suddenly much more receptive to Stella's charm than he had been just a little while ago. His feelings grew so intense that he was forced to relieve himself.

He pulled the chain on the toilet, then waited until the tank refilled and pulled it a second time. There was no longer the slightest trace of his sickness. He was glad of that.

His body seemed filled with a whole new store of energy, and he burst out laughing to himself, for no reason. He was certainly not going back to sleep now! If he woke up here in the morning, he would just be depressed again. He found his clothes, dressed silently, went over to the bed and kissed Stella lightly on the forehead, and then he left. The hard, dry cold in the street outside made him feel even better. He walked back to his apartment. Once there, he sponged himself off thoroughly, shaved, and dressed again. Seated on the edge of the bed, he waited for the proper moment to leave for his office.

He could hear the birds. There was always one that

began the concert, and then all the others joined in. Truthfully speaking, it was not really a concert. If you listened to it carefully, it was impossible not to notice the resemblance between this sound and that of a saw. A saw whose teeth were tearing painfully into wood. Trelkovsky had never understood why people insisted on comparing the noise of birds to music. Birds don't sing, they scream. And in the morning they scream in chorus. Trelkovsky laughed aloud. The mere idea of likening a raucous cry like this to a song must surely be the height of something-or-other—futility, no doubt. He wondered what would happen if men should suddenly adopt this practice of greeting the new day with a chorus of despairing screams. Even if only those with good reason for screaming were to take it up, it would still result in an unholy racket.

He heard a disturbance in the courtyard, unidentifiable at first, and then, very clearly, the sound of hammering. He went over to the window and looked down, but it was hard to see what was going on in the murky light of early morning. Then he knew what it was: they were repairing the glass roof.

9

The Petition

The concierge must have been watching for him to come in, because as soon as she saw him she signalled to him from behind the window of her room. Then she lifted a movable pane of the glass and called out, louder than was really necessary, "Monsieur Trelkovsky!"

She never managed to pronounce the s between the v and the k, so the name always sounded like "Trelkovky" He walked over to the window, smiling pleasantly.

"Have you seen Madame Dioz?" she demanded.

"No, why?" Trelkovsky didn't even know who Madame Dioz was.

"Never mind; I'll tell her that you're back. She wants to talk to you."

"What about?"

"You'll see, you'll see."

She slammed down the pane of glass, effectively cutting short the conversation, and bobbed her head up and down, just once, in a gesture that was more like a dismissal than a farewell. Then she turned back to the meal she was cooking on the stove, and paid no further attention to him.

Trelkovsky walked up the steps to his apartment, wondering vaguely what it was all about. He dropped his topcoat on the bed, pulled up a chair in front of the window, and sat down. He remained sitting there for a good half hour. He did nothing, and he thought of nothing specific, but simply passed in review the few unimportant episodes of the day which he still remembered. Snatches of conversation, actions of no real significance, faces glimpsed in the Metro or on the street.

After this, he stood up again and wandered from one room to the other until it occurred to him to pause in front of the little mirror he had hung on the wall just above the wash basin. He studied his reflection for some time, quite dispassionately, turning his head first to the left, then to the right, and finally lifting it so that he could observe the gaping cavity of his nostrils. Then, very slowly, he passed the palm of his hand over his entire face. His fingertips revealed the presence of a stiff little hair at the very tip of his nose. He brought his face up close against the mirror, searching for it. A little brown hair thrusting outward from a large pore. He went over to the bed, took a box of matches from the pocket of his coat, and very carefully selected two which seemed to have the sharpest, cleanest bases. Then he returned to the mirror and began trying to remove the hair, using the two matches as a makeshift tweezer. But the matches slipped, or else he hadn't got a good grip on the hair, because at the last moment it always got away. He was very patient, however, and in the end he succeeded. The hair was longer than he had thought it would be.

This much accomplished, he began squeezing idly at some blackheads on his forehead, but they didn't really interest him. He stretched out on the bed and closed his eyes, but he did not go to sleep.

He decided to tell himself a story.

"I'm on horseback, leading ten thousand maddened Zaporozhe Cossacks. For three days now, the frenzied hooves of our horses have thundered across the steppes. Ten thousand enemy horsemen are racing towards us, surging across the horizon with the speed of lightning. We don't turn an inch from our course; the shock of the two hordes, when they come together, can be heard for miles. I am the only one who remains in his saddle. I draw my scimitar and begin carving a path through the masses of men on the ground. I don't even look to see who receives the blows. I just cut and chop away. In a little while, the plain is nothing but a vast expanse of bloody remains. I sink my spurs into my horse's flanks, and he whinnies violently with the pain of it. The wind presses against my head like a tight-fitting helmet. Behind me, I hear the cries of my ten thousand Cossacks ... No, behind me, I hear ... No. I'm walking in the streets of a city, at night. The sound of footsteps makes me turn around. I see a woman, trying to escape from a drunken sailor. He snatches at her dress, and it tears away. The woman is half naked. I hurl myself at the brute and knock him to the ground with just the impetus of my charge. He does not get up. The woman comes up to me ... No, the woman runs off into the darkness ... No. The Metro at six o'clock in the evening. It's filled to overflowing. At every station, more people try to get into the cars. They push and shove the people who are already inside, supporting themselves against the doors and butting backwards with their rumps. I arrive, and give the biggest shove of them all. The whole crowd of people in the car bursts through its walls and falls onto the lines. The train coming in the other direction crushes the screaming mass of travellers. It goes on through the station in the middle of a river of blood ..."

Had someone knocked at the door? Yes, someone was knocking.

It must be the mysterious Madame Dioz.

The old woman who stood on the landing outside his door was a startling sight. Her eyes were bloodshot 'and heavily ringed, her mouth a straight, lipless line, and her nose very nearly touched the point of her chin.

"I have to talk to you," she announced, in a voice that was astonishingly clear and precise.

"Come in, madame," Trelkovsky said politely.

She marched unhesitatingly to the door of the second room, and glanced furtively around it, as if making sure that they were alone. Without looking at Trelkovsky, she handed him a sheet of ruled paper. He took it from her, and noted that it already bore several signatures. On its reverse side there was a short text, carefully written out in violet ink. It was a statement that the signatories were lodging a formal protest against a certain Madame Gaderian, who caused disturbances after ten o'clock at night. The old woman had lost interest in the apartment and was watching Trelkovsky, attempting to gauge his reactions.

"Well," she said. "Will you sign?"

Trelkovsky could feel the blood draining slowly from his face. How dare they suggest such a thing to him? Just to be sure he knew what they were preparing for him? They wanted to force his hand, and they were using black-mail to do it. This woman, whoever she was, first, and then he would be next, and if he refused to sign now he would be the first to suffer the consequences of his refusal. He looked for the signature of Monsieur Zy on the list. It was there, prominently displayed.

"Who is this Madame Gaderian?" he managed to say at last. "I don't know her."

The old woman's words came out in an angry whistle.

"She's the only thing you hear, after ten o'clock! She walks up and down, she moves things around, she does her dishes in the middle of the night! She wakes up everyone. She makes life impossible for all the other tenants."

"Is she the one who lives with a crippled daughter?" Trelkovsky asked.

"Nothing of the sort; she has a fourteen-year-old son. A good-for-nothing who amuses himself by hopping around the floor on one leg, all day long!"

"Are you sure? I mean—are you absolutely certain she doesn't have a young daughter?"

"Of course I'm sure. Ask the concierge. Anyone in the building can tell you."

Trelkovsky pulled himself up very straight. "I'm sorry," he said, "but I'm not signing any petition. This woman has never disturbed me; I've never even heard her. What apartment does she live in?"

The old woman evaded the question. "As you like," she said angrily. "I'm not forcing you to do anything. But if she wakes you up some night, don't come looking for me. It will be your own fault."

"Try to understand my point of view, madame," Trelkovsky pleaded. "I know you must have your reasons for doing something like this, and I don't want to cause you any difficulties, but I just can't sign it. Perhaps there is some reason why she has to do all of these things at night."

"Reasons—ha!" The old woman laughed disgustedly. "She has her reasons, all right—that's the way she is. She's a pest. There are always people who want nothing more than to torment everyone else. And if the others don't stand up and defend themselves, they end by walking all over them. Well, I have no intention of letting anyone walk all over me; I won't permit it. I'll go straight to someone who can do something about it. If you don't want to help us, that's up to you, but don't come complaining to me later. Give that back to me."

She snatched her precious sheet of paper from Trelkovsky's hand, and without so much as a word of farewell marched to the door, slamming it violently behind her.

"The bastards!" Trelkovsky raged. "The bastards! What the hell do they want—for everyone else to roll over and play dead! And even that probably wouldn't be enough! The bastards!"

He was so angry he was trembling. He went down to dinner in the restaurant where he always ate, trying to put it out of his mind, but when he returned to the apartment his fury was still pulsing through him. He went to sleep gnashing his teeth in helpless rage.

The next night, it was the woman with the crippled daughter who came to knock at his door, just before ten o'clock. She wasn't weeping this time. Her eyes were hard and cold, veiling a wicked glitter, but she seemed to relax a little when she saw Trelkovsky.

"Ah, monsieur!" she cried, "you see! I told you so. She's got up a petition against me! She has won! I'm going to be forced to leave. What a wicked, nasty woman! And they all signed—all of them, except you. I came to thank you. You're a good man, monsieur."

The girl was staring intently at Trelkovsky, just as she had the other night, and so was the woman now, her eyes glittering more fiercely than ever.

"I don't like this kind of thing," he stammered, confused and upset by the way they were watching him. "I don't want to get mixed up in it."

"No, no; it's not just that." The woman shook her head, as if she were suddenly very tired. "You're a good man. I can see it in your eyes."

She straightened abruptly and laughed. "But I got even!

The concierge is just as bad as she is, but I got even with her, too!"

She looked around her, assuring herself that no one could hear, and then went on, lowering her voice to a whisper. "Between the complaint and the petition, they've made me so nervous I got the colic. So you know what I did?"

The girl was still staring at Trelkovsky. He gestured feebly, indicating that he didn't know.

"I did it on the staircase!"

She laughed obscenely, but her eyes were hard with malice. "I did—on every floor, the whole length of the staircase. It's their fault; they're the ones who gave me the colic. But I didn't do anything in front of your apartment. I wouldn't have wanted to make trouble for you."

Trelkovsky was horrified. First by her story, and then by the lightning realization that, far from avoiding trouble for him, the absence of stains in front of his door could only more positively condemn him.

"How—how long ago?" he gasped.

She chuckled happily. "Just now. Just a minute or two ago. I'd like to see their faces when they find it tomorrow! And the concierge! She'll have to clean it all up! It's just what they deserve, all of them."

She clapped her hands together. He could hear her, still chuckling gleefully as she went down the steps. He leaned over the railings to see if she had been telling the truth. She had. A yellowish trail zigzagged down the line of the steps. He put his hands to his forehead.

"They're going to think I did it! I've got to do something—I have to!"

But he couldn't possibly start cleaning it all up now. He might be surprised by one of the other neighbours at any moment. He thought of doing it himself in front of his door, but he realized immediately that he couldn't, and

96

in any case the difference in colour and consistency would give him away. There might just be another solution.

Struggling to control his feeling of nausea, he found a piece of cardboard in the apartment and used this to gather up a little of the excrement from the steps leading up to the fourth floor. His heart was pounding violently against his ribs, he was bathed in fear and disgust, but he forced himself on. When he had finished, he dumped the contents of the piece of cardboard on the landing outside his door. Then he raced across to the toilet, to rid himself of the cardboard.

When he got back to his own apartment he was more dead than alive. He set the alarm clock to go off earlier than usual. He had no desire to witness the scene which would follow the discovery of what had happened.

But the next morning there was no trace of the events of the night before. A strong antiseptic smell rose from the still-damp wood of the steps.

Trelkovsky had his chocolate and two slices of dry toast in the café across the street.

Since he was early, he decided to walk to the office. He strolled through the streets unhurriedly, observing the passing crowds. The ranks of faces filed steadily, almost rhythmically before him, as if their owners were standing on some kind of endless moving sidewalk. Faces with the great bulging eyes of toads; pinched and wary faces of disillusioned men; round, soft faces of abnormal children; bull necks, fishlike noses, ferret teeth. Half closing his eyes, he imagined that it was really all one face, shifting and changing like the patterns of a kaleidoscope. He was astonished by the peculiarity of all these faces. Martians— they were all Martians. But they were ashamed of it, and so they tried to conceal it. They had determined, once and for all, that their monstrous disproportions were, in reality, true proportion, and their inconceivable ugliness was beauty. They were strangers on this planet, but they refused to admit it. They played at being perfectly at home. He caught a glimpse of his own reflection in a shop window. He was no different. Identical, exactly the same likeness as that of the monsters. He belonged to their species, but for some unknown reason he had been banished from their company. They had no confidence in him. All they wanted from him was obedience to their incongruous rules and their ridiculous laws. Ridiculous only to him, because he could never fathom their intricacy and their subtlety.

Three young men attempted to speak to a woman just in front of him. She said something very brief and sharp, and strode rapidly away. The men began to laugh and slap each other heartily on the back.

Virility was something else that disgusted him. He had never understood this business of vulgar pride in one's body and one's sex. They grunted and wallowed like pigs in their men's trousers, but they were still pigs. Why did they disguise themselves, why did they feel compelled to cover their bodies with clothing when everything they did reeked of the belly and the glands it harboured? He smiled to himself.

"I wonder what someone who could read my mind would think, if he were walking beside me now."

This was a question he often asked himself. Occasionally, he would even play at making up problems for the unknown mind reader to solve. He would say all kinds of things to him; sometimes telling him the truth about himself, and at other times just being crude and insulting. Then, as if he were talking on the telephone, he would pause suddenly in his narrative and listen for a reply. Quite obviously he never got one.

"He would probably think that I'm homosexual."

But he wasn't homosexual, he didn't have a sufficiently religious mind for that. Every homosexual is a sort of would-be Christ. And Christ, Trelkovsky thought, was a homosexual whose eyes were larger than his belly's appetite. People like that simply wanted to bleed for humanity; it was nauseating.

"I suppose I think that way because I am a man, after all. God knows what I might think if I had been born a woman ..."

He burst out laughing. But then the picture of Simone Choule on her hospital bed flashed before his eyes, and the laughter froze on his lips.

IO

The Fever

He was ill. For several days, he had not felt well. Cold chills raced across his back and up the length of his spine, his jaw trembled uncontrollably, his forehead burned one moment and was covered with an icy sweat the next. At first, he had refused to believe that anything was wrong, he had gone on as if nothing had happened. In the office he was forced to hold his head in his hands, trying to shut out the constant buzzing in his ears. If he had to climb a flight of steps, no matter how short, he was in pitiful condition when he reached the top. He could not go on like this any longer; he was ill, he was desperately ill.

Some kind of impurity had managed to work its way into the mechanism of his body, threatening to destroy it completely. But what was it? A mote that formed an obstacle to the proper functioning of two linked wheels? A gear that had somehow become unmeshed? A microbe?

The local doctor gave him no information as to the causes of the breakdown. He confined himself to prescribing a weak dosage of antibiotics, as a precautionary measure, and some little yellow pills that he was to take twice a day. He also recommended that he should eat a great deal of yoghurt. That had sounded like a joke, but the doctor shook his head vigorously.

"No, no," he said, "I assure you, I mean it. A lot of yoghurt. It will restore the condition of your intestines. Come to see me again in a week."

Trelkovsky called at the pharmacy on his way back to the apartment. He came out with his pockets full of little cardboard boxes which, in some manner, already gave him a feeling of reassurance.

As soon as he was safely at home he opened the boxes, took out the sheets of instructions and recommendations. and read them carefully. The medicines prescribed for him certainly seemed to possess some extraordinary qualities. But the next night he was no better. His cautious optimism was replaced with dull despair. He realized now that the medicines were in no way miraculous, and the notices in the boxes were nothing but advertisements. He had known it from the beginning, actually, but he had felt compelled to go on playing the game until he could prove that it was crooked.

He was in bed. He was very warm, but he felt that he was not warm enough. The upper sheet was pulled up around his nose, and he could feel a damp area where the saliva from his mouth had wetted it. He didn't have strength enough to blink his eyes. Either he lay there, holding them wide open, staring at nothing, or he drew a fleshy iron curtain across them, when the longing for oblivion became too strong. And even then, if he turned his head towards the window, the comfortable obscurity was tinged with a purple light.

He curled up in a ball beneath the covers. He was more acutely conscious of himself than he had ever been before. All of his dimensions were thoroughly familiar to him. He had spent so many hours observing and redesigning his own body that now he felt like someone who had just come across an unfortunate friend. He tried to constrict himself into the smallest possible space, so that the invading forces of weakness could find no room for a beachhead. His knees were drawn up almost into his stomach, the calves of his legs were tight against his thighs, and his elbows pressed hard against his ribs.

Above everything, it seemed imperative that he must find a manner of placing his head on the pillow so that he could not hear the beating of his heart. He turned and twisted over and over again before finally discovering one position that left him blessedly deaf. He could not bear to listen to that horrible sound, constantly reminding him of the fragility of his existence. It had often occurred to him that perhaps every man was accorded at birth a specific number of heartbeats, thus predetermining the duration of his life. When he realized now that, in spite of all his efforts, he could still hear the hesitant beating of his heart against his chest he took refuge beneath the covers. He pulled his head in under the sheet, and stared wildly at the outlines of his body, cowering in the gloom. Seen in this light, it took on a powerful, even massive, appearance. The sharp and penetrating animal smell it exuded fascinated him. He felt strangely calmer. He forced himself to break wind, so that the smell of his body would become even stronger, more unbearable. He remained beneath the covers as long as he possibly could, until he was on the verge of stifling, but when he finally emerged into the fresh air again he was strengthened. He felt more certain of the eventual outcome of his illness, a new peace of mind succeeded his earlier anguish.

That night, his condition grew worse. When he woke up, the sheets were soaked with sweat. His teeth were chattering. He was so thoroughly anaesthetised by the fever that he was not even afraid. He wrapped himself in a blanket and went to boil some water on a little electric plate that had belonged to the former tenant. When the water boiled he made himself a semblance of a hot drink, by pouring it through a strainer filled with tea leaves he had used before. He swallowed this, and took two aspirin tablets, and felt a little better.

He went back to bed, but as soon as he had turned out the light and was lying there in the darkness he was overcome by a feeling that the room around him was shrinking, growing smaller and smaller, until at last the walls formed a tight-fitting capsule around his body. He was suffocating. He reached out frantically for the light switch, and immediately the room returned to its normal dimensions. He inhaled deeply, trying to catch his breath.

"It's idiotic," he murmured.

He turned out the light again. The room sprang back at him like a taut elastic band when it is suddenly released. It surrounded him like a sarcophagus, weighing down his chest, circling his head, crushing in against the back of his neck.

In an instant he was suffocating, but fortunately his fingers located the switch at the last possible moment. His liberation was as sudden as it had been the first time.

He decided to sleep with the light on.

But it wasn't as easy as he had thought. The room did not change in its dimensions now—no, it was its consistency that was transformed.

More precisely, the consistency of the empty space between the furnishings.

It was as if this space had been flooded with water which then turned into ice. The space between the objects in the room had abruptly become as hard and solid as an iceberg.

And he, Trelkovsky, was one of those objects. He was imprisoned again. Not in a stone within the apartment this time, but in a void of space. He tried to move his limbs to shatter the illusion, but without success.

He remained a prisoner for more than an hour. It was impossible to sleep.

Suddenly, for no apparent reason, the phenomenon passed. The spell was broken. To make sure of it, he closed one eye. Yes, he could move again.

But the movement had unleashed a new sequence of events.

He had closed his left eye—very well—but in spite of the fact that his field of vision had been cut in half he had still seen everything! The objects in the room had simply moved over to the right. He closed his right eye, still not believing what had happened. The objects immediately moved over to the left. It wasn't possible! He selected two spots on the wallpaper as points of reference and blinked his eyes rapidly. But if he did not move his head he forgot the reference point he had chosen, and if he remembered the first one he couldn't find the second. He kept at it stubbornly, but in vain. And as a result of the effort of closing first his left eye and then his right he had an atrocious headache. His skull felt as though it had been put through a mangle. He closed his eyelids, but the picture of the room was still there. He could see as well as if the lids were made of glass.

The night, and its nightmare visions, drew to an end at last. Sleep came to his rescue, and did not leave him until late in the afternoon.

He heard the workmen in the courtyard, repairing the glass roof. He wanted to get up, but he was too weak. He thought he might be hungry.

Solitude revealed itself to him in all its horror.

No one to look after him, to pamper him, to pass a cool hand across his forehead and check on the course of his fever. He was alone, absolutely alone, just as though he were about to die. And if that should happen, how many days would it be before they found his body? A week? A month, perhaps? Who would be the first to enter his sepulchre?

The neighbours, no doubt, or the landlord. No one cared about him now, but it would be another matter when the rent came due. Even in death he would not be allowed to dispose freely of an apartment that did not belong to him. He tried to stem this depressing train of thought.

"I'm exaggerating; I'm not really so alone as all that. I'm feeling sorry for myself, but I know that if I just think about it ... Let's see ..."

He sought and sought, but no, he was alone, more alone than he had ever been. It was then that he realized the change that had taken place in his life. Why? What had happened?

The feeling of having an answer on the tip of his tongue upset him strangely. Why? There must be an answer. He had always been surrounded with friends, with relatives, with acquaintances of all sorts; he had guarded them jealously, precisely because he had known that there might be days when he would have need of them; and now he found himself alone, on a deserted island in the middle of a desert!

What a blind fool he had been! His mind refused even to recognize himself.

The hammering of the workmen in the courtyard drew him back from this gulf of self-pity. Since no one thought or cared about Trelkovsky, Trelkovsky must take care of himself.

And first, he must eat.

He dressed himself, not knowing quite what it was he was wearing. The descent of the staircase was terribly difficult. He wasn't conscious of the problem at first, but then the wooden steps transformed themselves into shelves of stone, rough-surfaced and unevenly joined. He stumbled against unexpected obstacles, bruised his body against sharp projections. And then countless little stairways began branching out from the main staircase beneath his feet. Tortuous little stairways, jungle stairways with bushy steps, stairways that turned inside out, so that it was impossible to tell whether you were on the exterior going down or the interior going up. In this labyrinth, he could find no way to guide himself, and he often lost his way. After having gone down one staircase that had suddenly reversed itself, he arrived at a ceiling. There was neither a door nor any sort of opening that would permit him to continue. Nothing but a smooth white ceiling, forcing him to lower his head. He resigned himself to turning around and starting over. But the staircase behaved as though it were balanced on an axis, like a seesaw, and when he arrived at a certain point that side went down and the other went up. It forced him to climb when he wanted to go down, and to go down when he knew he must climb.

Trelkovsky was terribly tired. For how many centuries had he been wandering these infernal corridors? He didn't know. He did know, vaguely, that it was his duty to go on.

Quite frequently, heads were thrust through the walls, observing him curiously. There was no expression on the faces, but he could hear laughter and the sound of sneers. The heads never stayed in place very long. They disappeared almost at once, but a little farther on other heads of the same kind would come out to look at Trelkovsky. He wanted to run along the walls with a gigantic razor blade in his hand, cutting off everything that projected beyond the stone, But unfortunately he had no such blade.

He was unaware of the fact that he had arrived at the ground floor. He went on with his interminable turning, going down, then climbing up. But at last he noticed the gaping hole in the unfinished roof of glass. The light made him shudder.

He could no longer remember why he had come out. His hunger was gone. He wanted only to be back in his bed. His illness must be more serious than he had thought. He managed to get back to the apartment without any great difficulty, but he had no strength left to take off his clothes. He pulled the sheets around him without taking off his shoes. But even like this his teeth were chattering.

When he awoke, it was night. He was no better, but the utter mindlessness of the fever had left him, giving place to an extraordinary sensation of lucidity. He got up quite easily. Still mistrusting his own reactions, he tried to walk a few steps, and found that he had no dizziness. It was more as though his feet were not touching the ground. This improvement at least permitted him to take off his clothes. He went over to the window to hang his trousers over the back of a chair, and automatically he glanced out at the oval window across the way. And in that room he saw a woman he recognized at once. Simone Choule.

She was sitting, in the position he had seen so often before, but then, as if she had guessed that he was watching her, she turned slowly in his direction. One hand went up to her face and she began undoing the bandage that covered it. She allowed only the lower half to be revealed, just up to the base of the nose. A hideous smile stretched the corners of her mouth.

Trelkovsky pressed his hands against his forehead. He wanted to tear himself away from this spectacle, but he did not have the strength.

Simon Choule was moving again. None of her gestures escaped Trelkovsky. He saw her lift her arm to pull the chain, make a final adjustment to her clothing, and then go out. The light in the toilet went dark.

Only then did he manage to turn away from the window. He went on taking off his clothes, but his fingers trembled when he tried to unbutton his shirt. He had to pull it open to get it off, and the cloth made a mournful sound as it tore. He didn't notice it. He was thinking of nothing but what he had just seen.

It wasn't so much the sight of Simone Choule's ghost that bothered him, since he was reasonably sure that his fever was responsible for that hallucination; but there had been another, even more bizarre sensation, while he was watching her.

For the space of several seconds he had thought himself transported across the courtyard and into the toilet, and from there he had been looking into the window of his own apartment. He had seen a face pressed against the glass, the face of a man who resembled him like a twin, and the eyes in that face had stared at him as if they were seeing a vision of unutterable horror.

11

The Revelation

The fever had passed, but Trelkovsky was finding it difficult to return to his normal way of life. As it receded, the
fever must have carried with it some particle of himself,
because now he had the feeling of being somehow incom-
plete. His blunted senses constantly gave him the impression of being out of step with his body. He was disturbed
by it.

When he got out of bed that morning he seemed to be
obeying a will that was not his own. He thrust his feet into
the slippers he always wore in the apartment, slipped a
bathrobe around his shoulders and went to boil some water
for his tea. He was still too weak to go back to the office.

When the water boiled, he poured it over the strainer
that held the tea leaves—fresh ones, this time. The liquid
in the cup was a beautiful colour, as delicate as some
Chinese inks, and with an aroma that was soft, discreet,
and yet irresistible. Trelkovsky never put sugar in his tea.
Instead, he put a lump of sugar in his mouth and then
drank the tea in little sips.

He could hear the hammering of the workmen repairing

the glass roof over the courtyard. Automatically, Trelkovsky put a lump of sugar on his tongue, took the cup in his hand and walked over to the window. The two workmen happened to be looking up at the time. When they saw Trelkovsky they burst into vulgar laughter. He thought at first that he was mistaken about it, that he was simply the victim of an optical illusion. But the truth of the matter was almost immediately apparent: the workmen were quite openly making fun of him. He was baffled, and then he became annoyed. He drew his eyebrows together in a frown, hoping to show them what he thought of their behaviour, but this produced no results whatever.

"It's too much," he thought. "What the devil do they think they're doing?"

He opened the window angrily and leaned out over the guard rail. The workmen began laughing even louder.

By this time Trelkovsky was trembling with rage. To such an extent, in fact, that the cup fell out of his hand. When he bent over to pick up the pieces, he heard another burst of noisy laughter. The workmen were apparently vastly amused by his clumsiness. When he looked out of the window again they were still watching him, smiling in a manner that was oddly nasty.

"What have I done to them?" he wondered.

Obviously, he had done nothing. But for some reason they were his enemies, and he could not imagine why he felt he could not tolerate it any longer.

"What's the matter?" he cried, pretending he had not understood what the men were doing. "What do you want?"

The loud, vulgar character of their laughter became even more pronounced. They watched for a few minutes longer and then went back to their work. But even with their backs to him, Tretkovsky was conscious of the smile that twisted their lips, and from time to time they glanced up at his window, shook their heads and muttered something to each other.

He felt as if he were rooted to the floor, petrified by his astonishment and anger, seeking vainly for a reason for what had happened.

"What on earth can it be? Why should they have started laughing the minute they saw me?"

He went over to the mirror and stared at his reflection.

But he was no longer himself.

He leaned closer to the mirror, and a muted scream of terror welled up in his throat. Then he fainted.

When he recovered consciousness some time later he realized at once that he had hurt himself in falling. He pulled himself painfully to his feet, and the first thing he saw was his image in the mirror—the face of a woman, heavily made-up. He could see it all now; the lipstick on his mouth, the rouge on his cheeks, the mascara on his eyes.

His fear became so tangible a thing that he could feel it forming a solid ball in his throat. Its surface was as sharp and rough as the teeth of a saw, tearing at his larynx. Why was he disguised like this?

He didn't walk in his sleep, he was certain of that. And where had the cosmetics come from? He began a frantic search of the apartment, and found them very quickly, in a drawer of the little chest. There were at least a dozen bottles of every size and colour, as well as tubes and jars of creams.

Was he going mad?

He snatched the bottles out of the drawer and hurled them against the wall, where they shattered noisily.

The neighbours promptly rapped on the wall.

So he was going mad, was he? He burst out laughing.

The neighbours rapped again, harder this time.

He stopped laughing. He was beginning to understand. And it was not funny.

His pyjama jacket was soaked with sweat, glueing to his skin. He collapsed on the bed, fighting with all his strength against the explanation that had come to mind. But he knew that it was useless; the truth was there in front of him, bursting across his vision like fireworks in a night sky.

It was their doing.

The neighbours were slowly transforming him into Simon Choule!

Using a thousand shabby little tricks, an unceasing vigilance, an iron determination, they were altering his whole personality. They were all in it together, they were all equally guilty. And he had fallen into their incredible trap like the innocent fool he was. They had disguised themselves and lied about each other, just to trick him. They had acted in this weird manner for no reason except to demoralise him and make him lose faith in his own intelligence. He had been nothing but a toy in their hands. When he thought back to all the details of his life in this apartment he realized that it had been that way from the very first. The concierge had called his attention to the window of the toilet the minute he stepped foot in this room. She had known all about the things that would happen there. And there was no point in wondering any longer who had cleared away the trash he dropped on the staircase. It was the neighbours.

It was also the neighbours who had robbed him, burning his bridges behind him, removing all possibility of a return to normalcy by depriving him of his past. And whenever his earlier personality showed signs of returning, it was the neighbours who rapped on the walls. They had made him abandon his friends, and forced him into wearing bedroom slippers and a bathrobe. It was a neighbour working in the café across the street who had made him drink chocolate instead of coffee, and smoke Gitanes instead of Gauloises. They had cunningly dictated all of his actions, all of his decisions. Nothing of himself had been left to him.

And now, taking advantage of the fever and his exhausted sleep, they had decided to strike a major blow. They had painted him to resemble a woman. But they had made a mistake this time; he wasn't quite ready for this. It had come too soon.

He remembered the thoughts he had had on the subject of virility. So that was it! Even his most private reflections had been imposed on him by others.

He took a packet of cigarettes from the pocket of the bathrobe and lit one. He was going to have to think about all this, as calmly as possible. And above everything, he must not lose his head. He inhaled deeply from the cigarette, watching the wisps of smoke drift upward from his nostrils. What about the landlord?

He was certainly the leader. He was the one who controlled all the movements of his pack of assassins. And the old woman, Madame Dioz? And the woman with the crippled daughter? Victims, like himself? Or neighbours? Neighbours, undoubtedly, charged with some inexplicable secret mission. And what about Stella?

Had she been warned that he would be coming to the hospital? Had she been sent there only to intercept him, to subject him to an influence he would have no reason to mistrust, because she had no connection with the apartment or the neighbours? He decided that, for the time being at least, he must believe in her innocence. He couldn't afford to see enemies everywhere he looked. He was not mad!

But what crime had he committed, that they should be

so intent on his destruction? Perhaps the same crime as that of a fly caught in the trap of a spider's web. The building was a trap, and the trap functioned. It was even possible that they had no personal animosity towards him. But when he thought of the stern, unbending faces of the neighbours, he abandoned this hypothesis. There could be no doubt of their personal animosity to Trelkovsky. They could not forgive him, just because he was Trelkovsky; they hated him for that, and they had determined to punish him for it.

Had this whole enormous machine been set in motion for no purpose except to punish him? Why such an effort, just for him? Had he done something to deserve it? Why should he be their chosen victim?

He shook his head. No, that wasn't possible. There must be something else.

Another question came to mind: was he the first victim?

And then another: was it really Simone Choule he had seen beneath the bandages in the hospital? And if not, how had they transformed her?

How long had the trap been functioning? How long was the list of tenants thus destroyed or transformed? Had they all chosen the same end as Simone Choule, or had some of them been charged with the task of perpetuating the deceased? Was this their way of reproducing themselves, of continuing their species? And in that case, had Simone Choule been a party to the conspiracy? Were they all some sort of creature produced from endless mutation, or were they simply murderers? Trelkovsky thought of the former tenant as he had last seen her, shrouded in bandages, her mouth gaping.

Would one of the neighbours commit suicide? Oh, no—Simone Choule was a victim, not an executioner.

He crushed the stub of his cigarette into the ashtray. Why? Why should they want to transform him?

Then his breathing stopped, his eyes opened wide with terror.

The day when he came to resemble Simone Choule completely, *totally*, he would be forced to do as she had done. *He would be forced to commit suicide.* Even if he had no wish to do so, he would have nothing to say about it.

He ran to the window. In the courtyard below, the workmen began to laugh as soon as they saw him. That was why they were repairing the glass roof! For him!

He felt suddenly dizzy, and put out his hand to catch at the chair, sinking back into it before he fell.

But he didn't want to die! This was murder! He thought of going to the police, but realized they would be no help to him. What could he say to convince a policeman of all of this, or to a superintendent who was a friend of Monsieur Zy's? But what else was there to do? Run away? Where to? Anywhere at all, it didn't matter, just get out of this building while there was still time. But he couldn't just throw away the money he had invested in the lease. There must be some solution. He sat by the window for a long time, thinking, and at last he found one that he thought might work.

He would have to go on for a little while longer, letting them think the transformation was taking place, so they would have no cause for suspicion. In the meantime, he would find someone else to take the apartment and then go off without leaving any new address.

There were two points to this solution which were not entirely satisfactory. The first was that the next tenant, coming into the apartment unwarned, would be the next victim; and the second was that the landlord might not give his consent to any transfer of the lease. It was impossible to do it without first notifying him. The ideal solution would have been to leave without notifying anyone —simply abandoning everything—but all of Trelkovsky's savings had gone into buying up this lease. He would have nothing left to fall back on. His only chance lay in gaining time, and money.

He decided to go downstairs and take a little walk through the streets of the neighbourhood, painted and scented as he was. He would have to put up with the jeers of the children and the contempt of the unknowing passersby, but this was the price he would have to pay if he wanted to cling to some hope of saving his skin.

PART THREE

THE FORMER TENANT

I 2

Revolt

Ever since Trelkovsky had become aware of the existence of a plot to destroy him, he had derived a morbid
pleasure from making the transformation of his character
as complete and perfect as possible. Since they wanted to
make him into someone else in spite of himself, he would
show them what he was capable of by himself. He would
beat them on their own ground. He would reply to their
monstrous plan with one of his own.

The shop he went into smelled of dust and soiled linen.
The old woman who ran it did not seem in the least astonished by Trelkovsky's appearance, and he decided that
she must be accustomed to this sort of thing. He spent a
good deal of time making a selection from the wigs she
brought out to show him. They were more expensive than
he had thought, but in the end he decided in favour of the
most expensive one she had. When he tried it on, it felt
like a headpiece of heavy fur. It wasn't at all disagreeable.
He left the shop without taking it off. In the breeze of the
street outside, the long strands of hair slapped gently against
his face, like the folds of a flag.

None of the passers-by seemed to pay any attention to him, although he had expected that they would stop and stare. He sought vainly for any trace of hostility in the way they looked at him. No—they were simply indifferent. And in fact, why should they be anything else? In what way was he interfering with them—with their right to do as they pleased, to behave in whatever manner they might choose? In his present ridiculous garb, he was less of an annoyance to them than others might be, because he was no longer a full-fledged citizen, he had renounced some part of his rights. His opinion was no longer of any importance. It was not a flag that slapped against his face, but an old sheet, covering and modestly concealing his shameful existence. Very well, since that was the way it was he would carry the thing to its logical conclusion. He would wrap his entire body in bandages, so that no one could see the leper he had become.

He went into another store and bought a dress, some lingerie and stockings, and a pair of very high-heeled shoes. Then he returned to the apartment, eager to put his plan into effect.

"As fast as I can," he told himself. "So that they can see what I've become because of them. So that they'll be frightened and ashamed. So they won't dare even look me in the face."

He ran up the staircase as fast as the remnants of his fever permitted. When he closed the door behind him, his curious sense of excitement exploded into an hysterical burst of laughter. But his voice was too deep, too masculine; he would have to practise speaking in falsetto tones. He amused himself for a time by murmuring idiotic little female phrases.

"Oh, but darling, she's not as young as she pretends to be; she was born the same year I was." Then suddenly, he cried, "I think I'm pregnant!"

The use of an adjective so distinctively feminine produced an extraordinarily erotic reaction. He repeated it over and over to himself, alternately whispering confidentially and speaking it aloud. "Pregnant . . . pregnant . . ."

Then he tried others. "Beautiful . . . Adorable . . . Goddess . . . Divine . . ."

He took the mirror down from the wall and stood it on the chest of drawers, so that he could follow the various stages of his transformation more closely. He was completely naked, except for the wig, which he had not wanted to remove. He got out his razor and shaving cream, and methodically shaved his legs from the ankle to the thigh. He pulled the girdle up over his hips, with the little wiggling motion he had seen women use, then pulled on the stockings, adjusted them carefully before attaching them to the little rubber snaps.

The mirror presented him with an image of his upper thighs and his genital organs, hanging down beneath the girdle. That annoyed him. He clamped them between his thighs, trying to conceal them entirely. The illusion was almost perfect, but in order to maintain it he was forced to hold his thighs tightly together and move only in tiny steps. He abandoned this for the moment and slipped on the transparent lace panties, which felt infinitely more pleasant against his skin than the shorts he normally wore. Then he fastened the artificially shaped brassière around his chest, and put on the slip and the dress. And finally, the high-heeled shoes.

It was the picture of a woman he saw in the mirror now. Trelkovsky was astounded. It was no more difficult than this to create a woman? He walked around the room, rolling his hips, trying to remember the way Stella walked. When he glanced over his shoulder and saw himself from the back, the image was even more real and more disturbing. He decided to imitate a number he had once seen on the stage of a music hall. With his arms crossed in front of him he clasped his waist with both hands, so that, from the back, an audience would have had the impression of a couple dancing. But it was his own hands that were caressing this strange woman. He shifted the position of the right hand until he was able to slip it beneath the neck line of the dress and unfasten the brassière. He was as tense and excited as if he were holding a real woman in his arms. Little by little, he removed all of the clothing, retaining only the stockings and the girdle when he stretched out on the bed ...

He was awakened by a searing pain whose source he could not at first identify. He wanted to scream, but the sounds became a gurgling bubble of blood. There seemed to be blood everywhere around him. The sheets were soaked with a mixture of blood and saliva. An intolerable aching throbbed in his mouth, but he dared not move his tongue to locate the roots of the pain. He staggered over to the mirror.

Of course! He should have expected this. There was a gaping hole inside his mouth—one of his upper incisor teeth was missing.

Sobs of pain and terror welled up in his throat, nauseating him. Without knowing what he was doing he was vomiting blood and weeping, lurching blindly from one end of the apartment to the other. His fear had become too great for him to contain, overflowing the limits of his consciousness, literally crushing him beneath its weight.

Who?

Had several of them come into the room, with one sitting on his chest to hold him motionless while the others rummaged in his mouth? Or had they delegated a solitary assassin to carry out the operation? And the tooth—where was it now?

He ripped off the blood-soaked sheets and the pillow case, looking for it, and then suddenly realized that there was no need to search. He knew where the tooth would be. He was so certain of it that he did not even attempt to verify it at once. First he stood at the wash basin and rinsed his mouth slowly and carefully. After that, he moved the armoire away from the wall and extracted the two incisor teeth from the hole behind it. They were both covered with blood, and although he rolled them about in his palm and examined them lengthily he could not tell which of them was his. He lifted his hand abstractedly to the side of his face, spotting it with red.

When did they plan to push him through the window? He should have known that acting as he had was dangerous. The more rapidly his transformation was accomplished, the sooner the execution would take place; he understood that only too well now. Instead of aiding and abetting the neighbours in their ghoulish work, he should be applying all of his strength to holding them back.

What a fool he had been! He had given them reason to believe that the process of metamorphosis was as good as completed, and they were so confident of themselves and their methods that they required nothing more. Instead of behaving as he had, he should have been demonstrating to them that there was still a good deal of work to be done before they could hope to achieve their goal. Making a Simone Choule of a Trelkovsky was not as easy as all that! He would prove that to them, very shortly.

He removed all trace of the make-up from his face, dressed in his own clothes, and went out. Was it simply a coincidence that Monsieur Zy opened his door just as he was passing? The landlord glanced at him irritably, and flicked one finger, presumably indicating that he wanted to talk to him.

"Tell me, Monsieur Trelkovsky," he said, "do you remember the conditions I mentioned to you when you first inquired about the apartment?"

Trelkovsky had all he could do not to hurl an accusation of his own crimes directly in the landlord's face. But he managed to control himself, and replied amiably, "Of course I remember, Monsieur Zy. Why do you ask?"

"You recall what I said about animals—dogs, cats, or any other kind of animal?"

"Certainly."

"What I said about musical instruments?"

"I remember that very well, Monsieur Zy."

"And what I said about women; do you remember that?"

"Naturally. You were very specific about that."

"In that case, why are you bringing women into the apartment?"

"But I've never brought a woman to the apartment!"

"Don't try to get away with that," the landlord snapped. "I know what I'm talking about. When I passed your door just a little while ago I distinctly heard you talking with a woman. Are you going to deny it?"

Trelkovsky was momentarily staggered. Could it be that the objective of the plot was simply to evict him from the apartment? No, that wasn't possible; there was more to it than that. But in that case, what did Monsieur Zy want of him now?

He shook his head. "I'm sorry, Monsieur Zy, but you're mistaken. There was no woman in my department. Perhaps I was singing; I don't remember."

"That wouldn't have been much better," the landlord said acidly. "But I distinctly heard a woman's voice."

Again Trelkovsky had to restrain the urge to fling his

knowledge of the truth at this man. But it was not so difficult this time; he was acquiring the habit.

"Anyone can make a mistake, Monsieur Zy," he said. "I would never go against your regulations by bringing a woman here. Perhaps you confused the sound you thought was coming from my apartment with the voice of someone else, on the staircase, or in another apartment. The acoustics in these old houses can play some very strange tricks!"

With that, he turned his back on the landlord and continued down the steps, congratulating himself on this final remark. If Monsieur Zy wanted to play games, he would show him that he could play too! He was undoubtedly on his way, right this minute, to tell the others that the victim wasn't quite ready for the scaffold. Trelkovsky had gained a small respite.

He walked over to the café across the street. The waiter nodded to him, and without asking what he wanted or waiting to be told brought him a cup of chocolate and two biscuits. Trelkovsky made no attempt to interfere until they were actually placed before him. Then he said that all he had wanted was a cup of coffee. The waiter looked at him in astonishment.

"But . . ." he said, gesturing at the cup, "you don't want chocolate today?"

"No," Trelkovsky replied firmly. "I said I wanted a cup of coffee."

The waiter went to talk to the proprietor, who was standing at the cash desk. He could hear nothing of their whispered conversation, but he saw them glancing constantly in his direction. The waiter came back at last, looking annoyed.

"I'm sorry," he said, "but the coffee machine isn't working. Are you sure you don't want chocolate?"

"I wanted coffee," Trelkovsky said, "but since that

seems to be impossible, bring me a glass of red wine. I don't suppose you have any Gauloises?"

The waiter shook his head and stammered something about being out of them.

Trelkovsky drank his wine slowly, enjoying it immensely, and then went back to his apartment.

The next morning there was a summons from the local police station in the morning mail. He assumed that it was something to do with the robbery, but the superintendent corrected this impression immediately.

"I've received several complaints about you," he barked, with no preface whatever.

"Complaints?" This was something for which Trelkovsky was totally unprepared.

"Yes, and don't look so surprised. I've been told a good deal about you, Monsieur Trelkovsky. Far too much, in fact. It seems you make a devil of a racket, every night."

"My God!" Trelkovsky blurted. "I'm sorry, superintendent, but you did surprise me. No one has ever said anything to me about this, and I'm not in the habit of making noise at night. I go to work every day and I have to get up very early. I have very few friends, and I never entertain at home. So you see, you did surprise me. You surprise me enormously."

"Perhaps," the superintendent shrugged, "but I'm not interested in that. I just know that I've received complaints about disturbances during the night. It's my duty to see that law and order are maintained in this district, so I'll tell you now, once and for all: stop whatever it is you are doing at night, Monsieur Trelkovsky. Trelkovsky—is that a Russian name?"

"I think so, yes," Trelkovsky murmured.

"Are you Russian? Are you a naturalised citizen?"

"No. I was born in France."

"Have you done your military service?"

"I was discharged because of an accident, superintendent."

"Let me see your identity card."

Trelkovsky produced the card from his wallet, and the
superintendent examined it carefully. When he handed it
back, his expression made it clear that he had hoped to
find something wrong with it.

"You haven't taken very good care of it," he said. "It's
torn."

Trelkovsky smiled mournfully, hoping that this would be
accepted as a form of apology.

"Very well," the superintendent said, "this time I'll let
you off with a warning. But don't let me hear any more
complaints about you. I can't let people who only think
of themselves disturb everyone else."

"Thank you," Trelkovsky said, "but I assure you, superintendent, that I am a very quiet person. I don't understand
this at all."

The superintendent waved him away. He had lost
enough time with him already.

Trelkovsky stopped at the concierge's on his way back
to the apartment. She had watched him approach the window without showing the slightest sign of recognizing him.

"I would like to know who registered a complaint about
me," he said. "Do you know who it was?"

Her lips came together in a tight line. "If you didn't
make all that noise, people wouldn't complain about you,"
she said. "You've got no one to blame but yourself. As for
me, I don't know anything about it."

"Was there a petition?" Trelkovsky insisted. "Was it
that same old woman who came to see me about the other
one? Did you sign it?"

The concierge turned away from him, deliberately

rudely, as if she could no longer bear the sight of him. "I told you I don't know anything about it. Now stop asking me questions; I have nothing more to say to you. Good night."

He would have to act quickly if he wanted to escape the neighbours. The net was rapidly drawing tighter. But it wasn't a simple matter. He tried to act perfectly normally, just as he had before, but he constantly caught himself in the act of doing things he would never have done before, of thinking in a manner that was not his. Already, he was not entirely Trelkovsky any more. But what was Trelkovsky? How could he learn the answer to that? He had to discover himself, so that he could be sure he would not wander from the right path. But how?

He no longer saw any of his old friends, and he never went to the places he had liked to go before. He had gradually become an indistinct shadow of a man, blotted out by the neighbours. And what they were constructing in the place of his own personality was the ghostly silhouette of Simone Choule.

"I have to find myself again!" he kept telling himself.

What was there that was uniquely his, that made him an individual? What was there that differentiated him from everyone else? What was his label, his point of reference? What was it that made him think: this is me, or, that's not really me? He sought the answers in vain, and was forced to admit at last that he didn't know. He tried to remember his childhood. He could recall the punishments he had received and some of the ideas that had come to him, but there was nothing unique or original in all that. The thing that seemed most important, because he remembered it so clearly, was an incident that could hardly be called a beacon light pointing to his identity.

Once, at school, he had asked permission to go to the

toilet, and because he was gone so long they had sent a little girl to see what had happened to him. When he went back into the classroom, the school teacher had looked at him and said, loud enough for everyone to hear, "Well, Trelkovsky, we were beginning to think you had fallen in!" His classmates had laughed and jeered. He had been scarlet with shame and embarrassment.

Was something like that enough to define him as a man? He remembered the sense of shame clearly enough, but he was no longer sure he understood the reasons for it.

13

The Old Trelkovsky

Scope and Simon were already seated in their usual places in the restaurant, near the radiator. They greeted Trelkovsky with boisterous shouts, calling to him from across the room.

"Well, look who's here! Have you decided to pay some attention to your friends at last? Where the devil have you been?"

Trelkovsky was annoyed and hideously self-conscious, but he went over to join them at their table. They had just started on their hors-d'oeuvre.

"Have you finally escaped from your neighbours?" they asked, almost in chorus.

He murmured a vague explanation of his absence, and sat down at the far end of the table.

"What are you doing, sitting there?" Scope said. "Don't you like your regular place any more?"

He had always sat on the banquette, with his back to the wall.

"Oh," he said, "yes, of course." He pushed back his chair and moved over to the banquette. He had completely forgotten this little detail.

"I hear you've been sick," Scope was saying. "I bumped into Horn, and he told me you hadn't been to work for a week."

Trelkovsky was staring at the menu, so he just nodded automatically and said, yes, that was right. The menu was written out in violet ink, and there were almost always mistakes in spelling in the names of the various offerings, furnishing a ready-made and continuing topic of conversation. The varieties of hors-d'oeuvre had not changed since he was last here. There was the traditional potato and herb salad, the home-made pâté, garlic sausage, and the raw vegetables—radishes, carrots, and the like. He felt a tremor of disgust. The old Trelkovsky would invariably have ordered a fillet of herring with some of the potato salad, but he knew that now he would be incapable of swallowing so much as a bite of it. Just this once, he would allow himself to cheat, to wander a little off the path. Scope and Simon were watching him, trying to pretend that they were not. They seemed enormously interested in what he was going to order. The waitress, a strapping Breton girl with a very pink complexion, came over to the table.

"We've missed you, Monsieur Trelkovsky," she said, banteringly. "Don't you like our food any more?"

He forced himself to smile, answering her in kind. "I was trying to get along without eating, but I've given up. It's too difficult."

She laughed dutifully, then immediately assumed an air of professional seriousness. "And what can I bring you, Monsieur Trelkovsky?"

Scope and Simon were literally hanging on his words. He swallowed desperately and blurted out, without a pause, "Some of the assorted raw vegetables, a steak with steamed potatoes, and a yoghurt."

He didn't dare look at the others, but he knew they were smiling.

"The steak medium rare, as usual?" the girl said.

"Yes . . ."

He would have liked to ask for it well done, but he didn't have the courage.

Scope was the first to break the silence. "What's happened to you?" he demanded. "You seem to have changed somehow."

Simon burst out laughing. He always laughed when he was on the point of making a joke. This time it had something to do with the fact that they had been talking about foreign exchange and now Scope said Trelkovsky had changed. He repeated it several times, to be sure they understood: exchange, changed . . .

Trelkovsky made an effort to laugh at himself. In vain. He was too preoccupied with the bits of cork or something or other that had fallen into his glass. He lit a cigarette and carefully arranged to drop the ash into it. The waitress brought him another glass.

As he ate, he tried to find something to say to the others. Something pleasant, a phrase that would at least show them he was still their friend. But he could think of nothing. The silence was becoming unbearable. He had to do something to break it.

"Have I missed any beautiful customers in here?" he asked, having had a sudden inspiration.

Scope winked at him. "There's one new one who is really something. Out of this world. She left just before you came in."

He turned to Simon. "And speaking of that, what's happening with Georges?"

"Oh, he'll get out of it all right," Simon answered, "but he'll never be able to work it the way he wanted to. You know that . . ."

From then until the very end of the meal, Scope and

Simon discussed this Georges and his incomprehensible manoeuvres. They laughed a great deal, but occasionally they also lowered their voices, as if to prevent Trelkovsky from hearing. If it hadn't been for this evidence of their mistrust of him, he would have thought they had completely forgotten him. He was relieved when he could at last leave them. Before they went their separate ways, they asked if he intended to come back the next day. Their uneasiness made him feel sorry for them.

"I don't think so," he said. "I'm very busy."

They made a convincing show of disappointment, but when they walked off they were laughing and talking delightedly. He watched them until they turned the corner.

He began walking slowly along the quays that border the Seine. In the old days, it was always here that he came when he had a few hours of freedom, just to stroll and to look at everything. But now the quays seemed mournful, and the Seine dirty. The book stalls were as repulsive to him as an endless row of garbage cans. Intellectual rag-pickers probed unconcernedly through all the refuse on display, searching for some morsel of spiritual nourishment. When they found it, an expression of animal-like cupidity crossed their faces, and they snatched it up as if some enemy were lying in wait to steal it from them.

This area depressed him too much. He crossed to the other side of the quay, but there he was confronted with the bird and pet market, with all the sounds and smells of caged animals. The idlers in the street were prodding at the turtles, teasing the parakeets, and doing their best to stir up the guinea pigs. Snakes were draped listlessly against the glass walls of their cage, and a little farther on a group of white mice observed their sinuous movements with rapt attention.

He walked for a long time. After having covered the

whole length of the walls of the Louvre, he went into the Tuileries gardens. He sat down on an iron chair near the great stone basin, so that he could watch the children sailing their little boats. They ran around the circle of water shouting to each other and waving the poles they used to guide the boats.

He noticed one little boy who had a power boat. A miniature ocean liner with two funnels and lifeboats all along the deck. The child was not one of the more active ones. He limped badly, and because of this he arrived at the opposite side of the pond some time after his boat was already there. It was this delay that caused the tragedy. A badly directed sailboat crashed into the side of the little ocean liner, which promptly capsized. It began to fill with water at once, and the unhappy child could only stand helplessly by, watching it as it sank. Tears ran down his cheeks in a steady stream. Trelkovsky expected that he would run to his parents for help, but he must have been alone because he just sat down on the ground and went on weeping. Trelkovsky derived a curious pleasure from his tears, as if they were a kind of vengeance for himself. He had the feeling that the child was crying for him, and watched happily as the tears formed in the corners of his eyes. In his mind, he was encouraging him, exhorting him to cry even harder.

But now some young, vulgar-looking girl was walking over to the child, bending over him, whispering something in his ear. The boy stopped crying, lifted his head towards the girl, and smiled.

Trelkovsky felt unbearably frustrated. Not only had the child stopped crying, he was actually laughing now. The woman was still whispering to him mysteriously. She seemed to be very excited about something. Her hands caressed the boy's cheeks and the back of his neck, she took hold of his shoulders and hugged him to her, and in the end she kissed him suddenly on the chin. Then she left him and went over to a wooden stall where an old woman was selling toys.

Trelkovsky left his chair and walked over to the child. He went out of his way to jostle him. The boy looked up, wondering what had happened.

"Rude little . . ." Trelkovsky hissed.

And without saying another word he slapped him twice across the face. He walked away rapidly after that, leaving the child crying again, overcome by the injustice of his fate.

He spent the rest of the day wandering through the streets of his old neighbourhood. When he was tired, he sat down on the terrace of a café and drank a glass of beer and ate a sandwich. Then he began walking again. He tried to remember, but he did not succeed. He paused at every street corner, hunting for memories of something, anything, that might have happened here, but he recognized nothing at all.

It was quite late when he came back to the building on the rue des Pyrénées. He hesitated at the thought of crossing the threshold of this gloomy place, but he was exhausted from his long walk and wanted only to sleep. He pressed the button that controlled the opening of the door. There was total darkness in the courtyard inside the door. The button for the light that would stay lit just long enough for him to get upstairs was somewhere on the wall to his right. He was extending an uncertain finger towards it when he was suddenly conscious of another presence, somewhere extremely close. He stood absolutely motionless, listening and waiting. Was someone breathing? No, it was himself. But he was still afraid to move his finger—afraid that it would encounter something soft or yielding; an eye, perhaps. He listened even more attentively. He couldn't just stand here like this; he had to do something. He held his arm out straight, taking a chance on the location of the button, and hit it right away. Light flooded through the entrance hall.

Sitting very close to him, on a refuse pail, a very dark woman was staring at him with demented eyes. He uttered a strangled cry. She gasped fearfully, and her lips began to tremble like the crackled surface of a glass of jelly. He wanted to get away, but his foot slipped on something on the ground and he lost his balance and stumbled towards her. Her body jerked with the violence of her effort to avoid him, and the cover of the pail rocked crazily. She fell backwards, screaming, and he screamed too as he fell on top of her. The refuse pail rolled over and its contents spewed out, almost burying them. The light went out.

He rolled over on the ground, trying to extricate himself. Something brushed against his face as it fled. He finally succeeded in getting to his feet. But in what direction should he run? Where was the button for the light now? Two claw-like hands encircled his neck and began to throttle him.

His tongue was bursting in his mouth, and he could hear the gurgling sounds of his own voice. Then something hit him on the head, very hard, and he lost consciousness.

He awoke in his apartment, stretched out on the bed. He was dressed as a woman, and he had no need even to look in the mirror to know that he was carefully made-up.

14

The Siege

He had been made ready for the sacrifice!

Because he had tried to escape, they were counter-attacking. And they had not hesitated to use outright aggression to achieve their ends. Whether he willed it or not, he was to be transformed into Simone Choule. They had left him no alternative.

Trelkovsky managed to stand up at last. He ached in every joint and his head was throbbing painfully. He dragged himself across the room to the wash basin and splashed cold water on his face. He felt a trifle more lucid after this, but the pain was still there.

The last act of the drama was already in progress. The climax must now be frighteningly close. He went over to the window, opened it, and peered out into the obscurity beneath.

The glass roof must be finished by this time. How were they planning to drive him to the point where he would kill himself? He did not want to die, but could that be considered a defeat for the neighbours? If their trap had functioned perfectly, Trelkovsky should really have transformed himself into Simone Choule and, like her, committed suicide completely spontaneously. But this was not the case; he had only been pretending, he knew very well that he was not Simone Choule. So what could they hope for now? That he would also pretend to die? He considered this solution for a moment. If he were to feign suicide—an overdose of barbiturates, for instance—would they be satisfied and allow him to go on living? The answer was almost certainly no. Illusion had no place in the dark plot in which he had been assigned the role of victim. The only possible climax was the destruction of the glass roof, pulverised by his shattered body.

What would happen if he should refuse to play his part, refuse to accept this as the only possible ending? The answer to this was no more of a mystery to him than the answers to his earlier questions. They would push him through the window. If suicide proved impossible, it would become murder. For that matter, there was no proof that the same thing had not been true in the case of the former tenant!

Down below him, the lights in the courtyard had suddenly gone on. The sound of a galloping horse's hooves broke into the silence. Trelkovsky leaned forward a trifle, wondering what could be happening.

He was astonished to see that a man on horseback had actually ridden into the courtyard. He could not make out his features, because he was wearing a mask over his eyes, and a broad-brimmed hat of deep red felt cast the lower part of his face into shadow. A body was slung across the horse's rump, hanging face down. Trelkovsky could not be sure, but he had the impression that its hands and feet were bound.

The courtyard was swarming with people now. Groups of neighbours surrounded the masked stranger, seeming to converse with him by unintelligible signs and gestures. A woman with a pale blue shawl across her shoulders pointed to Trelkovsky's window. The man dismounted and walked around his horse, moving slowly to a point directly beneath. He cupped his hand across his forehead, as if there were a strong sun, and stared up at Trelkovsky. A boy wearing short, olive-green pants, a yellow-brown sweater and a mauve beret walked up to him and ceremoniously held out an enormous black cape. The man adjusted it on his shoulders, and then disappeared through the arch that led to the entrance hall. The rest of the people in the courtyard followed him, leading the horse, which still carried the inert form of the prisoner. The lights went out.

Trelkovsky might have thought he had been dreaming, but he knew that he had just witnessed the arrival of the executioner. He was undoubtedly climbing the steps to the apartment at this very moment, unhurriedly, moving with the same deliberate pace with which he had crossed the courtyard. He would simply throw open the door, not waiting for any invitation, and walk into the room, with all the calm detachment of a man going about his normal daily work. Trelkovsky knew what that work would be. In spite of his cries and pleas for mercy, he would be hurled out into the void. His body would crash through the glass roof, splintering it to a million fragments before being crushed on the ground.

Panic seized him, plucking him from his apathetic resignation. He raced over to the armoire, his teeth chattering wildly, and began pushing and pulling at it, struggling to move it into position in front of the door. Sweat rolled down from his forehead, blinding him, leaving black streaks of mascara running down his face and onto his neck. The dress they had clothed him in hampered his movements, so he ripped it off and tore open the fastenings of the brassière. As soon as the armoire was in place he ran back to the window and blocked any entrance through it with the chest of drawers. His lungs seemed about to burst, his breathing was no more than a despairing croak.

Someone knocked on the door.

He had no intention of answering, but he dragged two chairs across the room to reinforce the armoire.

The neighbours upstairs pounded on the ceiling.

All right, he *was* making a racket this time! They could go ahead and pound! If they thought for a minute that they could force him into surrender that way, they were sadly mistaken!

The pounding on the floor beneath him was coming from the landlord.

They were all in it now! But they were wasting their time. Trelkovsky was not going to be influenced by their pounding any longer. He would barricade himself in this room, in spite of them or anything they did.

The knocking at the door was becoming more violent, but he paid no attention to it and went on establishing his system of defences, utilising everything he could find. He discovered a ball of heavy twine in the bottom of a drawer and used it to tie the armoire and the chairs together, making one unit of all of his separate elements. He did the same thing with the chest of drawers and the other objects he had placed in front of the window. As he worked, he heard something strike against one of the panes, and the sound of breaking glass. If they tried to get in through here, they would be too late!

"You're too late!" Trelkovsky screamed. "And I hope you kill yourselves getting down!"

Another pane of the window broke. They were throwing stones at them.

"I'll defend myself, I warn you! I'll defend myself to the

end! It's not going to be a game, you hear me! I'll sell my skin dearly! I'm not a lamb you can just lead to the slaughter!"

The reaction to his outburst was immediate. The pounding on the walls and the door stopped. There was silence everywhere.

They must be holding a conference about what to do next. With some difficulty, Trelkovsky managed to climb inside the armoire and place his ear to the wall at its back. He was close enough to them this way, but he could hear nothing of their conversation. He clambered out and sat down on the floor in dead centre of the front room, all his senses alert and waiting. The minutes passed, interminably, but there was no sign of life from the neighbours. Could they have gone away?

He smiled. That trap was a little too obvious! They were just waiting for him to open the door. But there was no danger of that. He was not going to move a finger.

After two or three hours of silent, motionless waiting, he noticed the sound. The sound of water dripping slowly from a leaky tap. At first he tried to ignore it, but the sound became too irritating. He stood up very slowly, and went over to the basin, walking as softly as he could. His fingers reached out to touch the tap, and found it perfectly dry. But the moment he turned his back, the sound began again. In order to be absolutely certain, he held his hand beneath the tap, listening intently. The dripping sound continued. It was coming from somewhere else.

He made a complete circuit of the apartment, studying the walls and ceiling, searching for the origin of this persistent, nagging sound. He found it very quickly. Drops of some brownish liquid were filtering through one of the cracks in the ceiling of the back room. At varying intervals a single heavy drop would form, lengthen into a tear and fall, splashing into a little puddle formed on the floor by the drops that had fallen before. The moonlight through the single uncovered chink of the window gave the puddle the appearance of a precious stone, a deep red ruby. Trelkovsky lit a match and bent down to study it. Yes, the liquid was a reddish colour. Blood?

He dipped a finger in it and then rubbed the finger against his thumb, trying to gauge the consistency of the liquid. This operation, however, told him absolutely nothing. He decided, against his will, that he would have to taste it. But he learned very little from that—it had almost no taste.

He remembered then that it had rained a great deal in the past few days. Perhaps there was a leak in the roof ... But this explanation seemed hardly feasible. There were three other floors between the roof and his ceiling. Of course, it was possible that water had worked its way down through some kind of continuing crack. That might be it ...

But suppose it was the blood of the prisoner he had seen slung across the executioner's horse in the courtyard? Suppose his mutilated body had been left on the floor of the apartment above, just so that this would happen, so that Trelkovsky would know the fate that lay in store for him?

The drops were falling more regularly now, the puddle was growing larger. Ploc! Ploc! The miniature waves rolled out across the dry surface of the floor, rhythmically, steadily, like an incoming tide. Could they be planning to flood the apartment, to drown Trelkovsky in blood!

And what was this sound that had begun to echo the dripping from the ceiling? He went back to the wash basin. The tap must somehow have loosened, because drops of liquid were falling steadily from it too. He tried to tighten it, hammering at it with his fist, but it was impossible. How could the washer have given out from one minute to the next, when the tap was not even turned on?

The two leaks seemed to be answering each other, creating the illusion of a dialogue between the two liquids.

The ticking of the alarm clock had become incredibly loud, and Trelkovsky was suddenly conscious of the fact that the dripping sounds were synchronised with its steady ticking. He picked up the clock, intending to stop it, and then dropped it angrily on the bed and covered it with a pillow. There is no way to stop an alarm clock except by breaking it.

Someone knocked at the door. The neighbours were returning to the attack. He glanced hastily around him, checking the condition of his fortifications. They seemed satisfactory. There was, however, that one unprotected chink at the window, because the chest of drawers was not quite wide enough to cover it completely. A very small form—a child or a monkey, for instance—might be able to get in through there. The thought worried him; there was no telling what these people would attempt.

And then, just as he was staring at the narrow opening, wondering what he could do about it, he was horrified to see a tiny hand, brown and very hairy, reach through one of the broken panes and grasp the base of the framework. He seized the only kitchen knife he possessed and began hacking desperately at the thing. There was no sign of blood, and after a minute or two the hand released its grip on the sill and vanished. He waited for the sound of something falling on the glass roof, but all he heard was a burst of sardonic laughter.

He realized then that the neighbours in the apartment beneath could very easily have placed a glove on the end of a long pole and lifted it up to his window, simply to frighten him. He put his eye to the open space between the chest of drawers and the wall, trying to see what was going on in the courtyard.

The neighbours had apparently used the stratagem of the

glove on the pole simply to attract his attention, because they were obviously waiting for him. They had prepared an extraordinary spectacle, and the moment he saw it he was convinced that its sole objective was to drive him out of his mind.

A large number of wooden packing cases were strewn around the courtyard. They were stacked on top of each other at differing heights, so that they looked like the rows of sky-scrapers on postcards of New York. And on top of each of the piles of cases squatted one of the neighbours. Some of them were directly facing him, others in profile, and still others sat with their backs to him. From time to time they pivoted slowly, changing their positions without seeming to move their limbs at all. Suddenly, an old woman stood up, and Trelkovsky recognized her at once as the Madame Dioz who had tried to get him to sign her petition. She was wearing a long, violet-coloured dress, cut so low that it revealed the whole upper part of her withered breasts. She raised both her arms towards the sky and began a heavy, awkward kind of dance, leaping clumsily from case to case. Each time she jumped from one to another she let out a raucous scream. "Youp!" she screeched, and then leaped into the air. "Youp!" and she leaped again.

This ritual lasted until the bald neighbour sitting on the tallest pile of cases stood up and began swinging a heavy bell that gave out a deep and echoing sound. The neighbours then hurriedly descended from their perches and disappeared, carrying the cases with them. The boy who had handed the black cloak to the executioner suddenly appeared in the deserted courtyard. He was carrying a long pole over his shoulder, and at the end of the pole hung a cage containing a live bird. A woman clothed in a flowing red chasuble trotted behind the boy, with her face thrust close against the bars of the cage. She was waving her arms in the air, imitating flight, and making hideous little chirping sounds, trying to frighten the bird. The boy made a complete circuit of the courtyard without once turning around to look at her.

After these two came the pregnant women, their faces daubed with every shade of red, old men riding on the backs of other old men on their hands and knees, rows of little girls, gesturing lewdly, and dogs as big as young steers.

Trelkovsky clung to reason as tightly as though it were a lifeline. He recited the multiplication tables to himself, and when he had exhausted that he began on the fables of La Fontaine. He set himself to accomplishing difficult movements with his hands, verifying the proper co-ordination of his reflexes. Speaking aloud, pretending he was giving a lecture, he even drew up a complete picture of the political situation in Europe at the beginning of the nineteenth century.

Morning came at last, and with it an end to the witchcraft of the night.

As soon as he dared, Trelkovsky removed all trace of the make-up on his face, changed the remnants of the female clothing he still wore for his own, and moved the armoire away from the door. He raced down the staircase as fast as his feet would carry him, never even glancing to either side. Once, a hand reached out, trying to hold him back, but he was moving so fast that it failed to get a grip on his shoulder. He passed the concierge's room at a dead run, and began running even faster as soon as he was in the street.

A bus was stopped for a red light just ahead of him. He leaped onto the rear platform at the very moment it started off.

He would forget about the lease, and about the savings he had exhausted to pay for it. His only chance of safety, now, lay in flight.

145

15

Flight

To flee, to get away—that was all very well—but where?

Trelkovsky went through a feverish review of every face he had known, trying to discover the one that might come to his aid. But they all seemed curiously cold, indifferent, or forbidding.

He had no friends. There was no one in the entire world who cared. No, that wasn't true—there were people who cared about him, but what they wanted was only his madness and death.

Why should he try to save himself, when the effort was clearly useless? Wouldn't it be preferable simply to extend his neck to the executioner? He might spare himself vain and endless suffering. He was terribly tired.

One name flashed through his mind, bright and shining as the headlights of a car on a lonely road at night. Bright and shining as a star.

Stella.

She would not reject him, not Stella. She would simply ask him in, with no reticence, no foolish words. He was swept by a feeling of infinite tenderness for this girl, and his eyes filled with tears. Poor little Stella! So soft, so feminine, and as much alone in the world as he was himself. Stella, his guiding star.

He had a sudden mental picture of her, walking alone on a cold, deserted beach. The sea was lapping at her feet. She was walking very slowly, as if she were in pain; she must be extremely weary. Poor little Stella—how far had she had to walk like this? And now there were two men on the beach, wearing boots and helmets. Without saying a word, they went up to the solitary figure of the girl, their whole attitude betraying their arrogance and unconcern. She understood their intentions at once. She began to plead with them, she fell on her knees, imploring them for mercy, but they simply stared down at her, unmoved by her tears and cries. They took out their revolvers and fired several bullets into her head. The frail body collapsed on the sands, curled up into a tiny ball, and then was motionless. Stella was dead. The waves washed across her legs and the hem of her skirt. Poor Stella!

Trelkovsky was so overcome with pity that he was forced to hide his face in his handkerchief, attempting vainly to stem the flow of tears. Yes, he would take refuge with Stella.

He wandered through the neighbourhood where she lived for a long time, because he could not remember the name of her street.

By the time he found it he was far less certain of his welcome than he had been at first. It was possible that she might not be at home. He had visions of standing in front of a closed door, after having climbed the stairs and knocked, consumed with hope and the thought of safety at last. And there would be no one there. He would knock and knock again, unable to convince himself that there was no

THE TENANT

longer any hope. He would not dare go away, for fear she
might open the door after he had left.

He told himself that he must try to imagine every possible eventuality, so that fate could not take him by surprise. It was an old and firmly rooted belief of Trelkovsky's that fate only intervened in cases of utmost
emergency. Thus, if you could foresee misfortune and
plan ahead, it could be avoided. He set himself to con-
sidering all of the possibilities.

She might not be alone. She would open the door, just
enough for him to see that she was lightly draped in a robe
or dressing gown, and would not ask him to come in. He
would be left standing on the threshold, fidgeting with
embarrassment, not knowing what to do next. And finally
he would turn and run away, scarlet with confusion, angry
with her and with himself.

She might also be ill, and there would be members of
her family or friends staying with her. She would not
recognize him, because of the fever, and the others would
regard him suspiciously, as if he were some kind of crim-
inal intent on taking advantage of a helpless girl.

It was not at all impossible that the door would be
opened by a man or a woman he had never seen before.

"Madame Stella, if you please," he would ask timidly,
and the stranger would reply, "Stella? I don't know anyone by that name. Stella who? Oh—the other tenant! She
left yesterday. No, she won't be coming back. She's moved
—we're the new tenants. No, I don't know her new
address."

As it turned out, however, it was Stella herself who
opened the door for him. There were little flecks of yellowish matter caught in the corners of her eyes, and her
whole appearance somehow conveyed a smell of a bedroom and of dried sweat. She held the two ends of her

dressing gown around her with one hand, while the other still rested on the doorknob.

"Am I disturbing you?" he said stupidly.

She shrugged slightly. "No. I was sleeping."

"I wanted to ask if you could do me a favour."

"What?"

"Could I stay here with you for two or three days? I wouldn't be any trouble, but if you can't do it, just say so. I wouldn't blame you."

Stella lifted a finger to clear the yellowish matter from her eyes, and stared at him in surprise. Then she shrugged again. "No," she said, "it wouldn't be any trouble. Are you having problems?"

Trelkovsky nodded. "Yes. Nothing serious, though. It's just that I don't have an apartment any more."

"You haven't slept tonight," Stella said, and smiled. "You look tired. I'm going back to bed myself—if you want to sleep . . ."

"Yes, thank you . . ." he murmured, abruptly conscious of his exhaustion.

He undressed slowly, as slowly as possible. Dear, sweet little Stella! He wanted to savour the simplicity and kindness of her presence. She had acted exactly as he had hoped she would. When he took off his socks he noticed that his feet were dirty.

"I'm going to freshen up a little," he said, but she was already back in bed.

When he joined her there, her eyes were closed. Was she really sleeping? Or had she wanted him to know that she was allowing him to sleep here, but only to sleep? His uncertainty was of short duration, because a moment later her soft hands were caressing his body. He wrapped his arms around her gratefully, holding her very close.

When she got up next morning, he opened one eye, more

for courtesy than any other reason. She kissed him lightly on the ear.

"I have to go to work," she whispered. "I'll be back about eight o'clock tonight. It would be better if the neighbours don't see you. If you go out, try to do it without being seen."

"All right," he said.

Then she was gone, and he was instantly wide awake, freed of any further need for sleep. He had done it! He was saved! He had an overpowering sense of well-being and security. He made a complete tour of the apartment, smiling blissfully at everything he saw. It was delightful here; it was neat, tidy, and reassuring. He spent the day reading and continuing his exploration of Stella's private domain. He didn't go out at all, not even to eat. He would have had to be a complete fool to leave this miraculous haven!

Stella came back at seven-thirty, carrying a string bag filled with provisions. Two bottles of wine clinked cheerfully together in its recesses, as if they were toasting each other.

"I don't have the time to do any real cooking," Stella explained as she took off her coat, "so I always buy tinned things. I'm a great chef with tins!"

He watched her as she began preparations for their dinner, feeling so filled with tenderness for her that he was almost sad.

"I adore tinned things," he murmured, and after that he contented himself with just watching her as she came and went in the room. He was thinking of her thighs and her breasts. And to think that she had put all of this at his disposition, with no attempt at bargaining or haggling. He remembered the line of her back and her shoulders, finding it hard to believe that all of this body was actually there, occupied with preparing his dinner. Adorable Stella!

He wondered why he could not remember her navel, and closed his eyes, trying to call up a picture of it. In vain. He had forgotten it.

She was setting the table, and her back was momentarily turned to him. He walked up to her, very quietly, and surprised her with a kiss on the shoulder. His hands imprisoned her breasts and then moved slowly down along her sides as he turned her around to face him. He found the opening that separated her sweater from the skirt, and the snaps that held the skirt yielded one by one to his insistent pressure. His eyes were on a level with her navel now. He kissed it passionately, and then studied it for a long time, wanting to engrave every detail of it in his memory. She leaned forward slightly to see what he was doing. She had certainly thought that his intentions were quite different, and he had no wish to deceive her.

The next day, while Stella was at work, someone knocked at the door. He did not go to open it, but the visitor refused to be discouraged. He simply went on knocking, at the same regular cadence, with no appearance of impatience. The sound became exasperating. Trelkovsky got down on his hands and knees and crawled over to the door, peering anxiously through the keyhole. He could see nothing but a small square of an overcoat, buttoned over a fairly portly figure. It was a man.

"There's no one home?" he heard the visitor say.

The blood seemed to drain from Trelkovsky's face, his neck, even his shoulders, leaving him white and shaken.

He had recognized the voice. It was Monsieur Zy!

So they had followed him!

Impossible! He had taken all kinds of precautions. What could have happened? Did Monsieur Zy know Stella personally? And he didn't know that Trelkovsky had taken refuge with her? But in that case, he would certainly learn about it, even though Stella did not know his address and had no reason to suppose that he knew Monsieur Zy. Unless . . .

He shuddered.

Suppose it was Stella who was responsible—suppose Stella had cold-bloodedly betrayed him, to punish him for having lied to her about the apartment? But how could she have learned his address? He clapped a hand to his mouth, just in time to stifle a cry of rage. In his pockets! She had gone through his pockets, the little cheat!

There would surely have been one or two letters, and that would have been enough to tell her everything. She had been a friend of Simone Choule's, she probably knew the neighbours, so she would have understood what Trelkovsky's 'problems' really were. She had betrayed him to get revenge.

That must be it, because if Monsieur Zy actually did know Stella, he would know that she worked during the day and there was no one in her apartment then. He had come here solely because of Trelkovsky . . .

The hypothesis he had fleetingly considered, and then rejected, was the correct one after all. Stella was one of the neighbours!

She had been charged with his capture from the very beginning, ordered to lead him back to the slaughter! The mere thought of it frightened him. It was too monstrous, too horrible to be believed. But the more he thought of it, the more it seemed the obvious solution. He had been trapped from the first. And what a fool he had been!

Standing here whispering, "Poor little Stella—dear little Stella!" He should have bitten off his tongue. He had felt sorry for someone who was trying to kill him! Why hadn't he felt sorry for Monsieur Zy and all the rest of the neighbours, while he was at it?

When he thought of his tenderness towards the girl— she must have had a good laugh from that, the little whore! And for all he knew, she might even be the one who had murdered Simone Choule. And she said she was her best friend!

Monsieur Zy had finally stopped knocking. Trelkovsky listened to the sound of his footsteps, hesitant at first, as if he could not quite make up his mind to leave, seeming to turn back, and then vanishing.

He would have to flee, again. But what would he do about money?

Furiously, he set to work searching Stella's apartment, pulling out the drawers of the chest, hurling the mattress on the floor, ripping the photographs and prints from the walls. He found some money hidden away in an old handbag. Not very much, but enough to go to a hotel. Without a shadow of remorse, he stuffed it all into his pocket. The little bitch deserved worse than this!

He opened the door as noiselessly as possible, and explored the landing and stairway before venturing out. Everything seemed to be perfectly normal, and a few seconds later he was out of the building and safely in the street.

To elude any possible pursuers, he took several different taxis, and when at last he was certain that no one could have followed him he went into the first hotel he saw. It was the Hotel des Flandres, located just behind the Gare du Nord.

He signed a false name to the hotel register—Monsieur Trelkof, from Lille—but fortunately no one asked for his identification papers. He began to breathe a trifle more easily. Perhaps he could find some way of escaping them, even now.

16

The Accident

Trelkovsky paced up and down in the room, like a caged animal. Occasionally, he went over and peered through the window, which looked out on a kind of deep pit with walls pierced here and there by windows. The room was on the sixth floor, but received little direct light, since all of the surrounding buildings were taller than the hotel. For the rest of the day, he went out only to go to the toilet, which was down at the end of a gloomy corridor. He went to bed very early.

He woke up in the middle of the night, of course, his body cold and damp with fear. He had had a whole series of horrible nightmares. Lying in bed with his eyes open, he searched the shadows around him, trying to find some steadying, reassuring objects. But the reality was at least as threatening as the nightmares. Having swallowed up all the familiar shapes of the furniture, the darkness took on the aspect of some unearthly challenge: within this nothingness something monstrous and unknown was surely being spawned.

The room had become a kind of breeding ground for

monsters. For the moment, nothing specific could be detected, but that would not last. Like a communicating vessel in a chemist's laboratory, Trelkovsky's overflowing brain would spill its terrors into the void of the room, and as they passed from one recipient to the other they would take form and substance. The monsters Trelkovsky had foreseen would be living organisms, preparing to feed on their creator. He must not go on thinking like this; it was too dangerous.

By the time morning came, he had made up his mind that he must somehow acquire a weapon.

This was easy enough to say, but how was he to obtain it? He had read enough mystery novels to know that he would have to have a permit to carry a gun. Any arms shop he might go to would ask for it before he had a chance to finish his question, and when they found he did not have it they would simply refuse to sell to him. It was even possible that they would tell him to follow them to the nearest police station, or detain him in the shop on some pretext until the police could get there. And as for going to the police station and requesting the issuance of a permit to him, how would he justify it? If he reported the details of the neighbours' plot against him, they would think he was crazy. They might even try to send him to an asylum.

It would be far wiser to do nothing through official channels.

He left the hotel, walking close in the shadow of the walls, and began a circuit of all of the shadiest-looking bars in the neighbourhood. In every one of them, he almost succeeded in forcing himself to ask the barman if he had a pistol he would sell him, but in the end he didn't dare. He paid his bill rapidly, slunk out like a thief, and made a new attempt in the café next door or across the street. In the early afternoon, he gave up. He was slightly drunk, because he had been drinking some kind of alcohol in every place he went into, trying to achieve the air of a man accustomed to this sort of thing. He had eaten nothing in the past twenty-four hours, and the alcohol had gone promptly to his head.

As a last resource, he decided to buy a toy pistol. He had heard that some of these children's playthings could do a great deal of damage. There were constant stories in the newspapers to prove it. He remembered one that told about a little boy who had been blinded by just such a toy. If that kind of result could be obtained by accident, it should be a simple matter for him to do better. The saleswoman in the department store explained the workings of the little pistol to him. He tossed aside the box it came in and slipped it in his pocket. The saleswoman watched him leave, smiling and shaking her head indulgently.

He felt greatly reassured by the presence of the weapon. He held his hand tight against his pocket, feeling its form moulded to his palm through the cloth. He wanted to take it apart, and also to try it out, at once, but he could hardly do this in a public street, since other people might not realize that it was just a toy. He had to get back to the hotel, as quickly as possible.

The sound of shouting brought him suddenly back to reality. He sensed that some kind of danger was threatening him, and thrust his hand into his pocket, but had no time to withdraw the pistol. The shock of impact threw him several feet. He felt the heat of the radiator grill against his body, but the car had stopped in time.

It was a big American car, though not very new. The chromework was tarnished, one of the headlights was broken, the paint was flaking off in spots, and one of the fenders was newly dented.

"That must have happened when it hit me," Trelkovsky thought. "I just hope there won't be any trouble about it."

He wanted to laugh, but the effort hurt too much.

People were running up from every direction, pushing and shoving in a circle around him. They had not yet dared touch him, but it doubtless wouldn't be long before they did. They were avid for details on the exact extent of the damage. Trelkovsky was glad he had remembered to wash his feet. That would spare him embarrassment when they took him to the hospital. A man was pushing his way determinedly through the crowd.

"I'm a doctor," he called. "Let me pass. Get out of the way, will you, he needs air."

Trelkovsky kept his teeth tightly clenched while someone examined him cautiously. The doctor was trying to get him to speak.

"Are you in pain?" he kept asking. "Can you hear me? Where does it hurt? Can't you talk?"

Why should he bother to talk? It was delightful not to have to answer when someone spoke to you. And besides, he was completely amorphous, incapable of the smallest effort.

He contented himself with waiting to see what happened next, not even feeling curious about it. It was all something of no concern to him. His head was turned so that he could see the car that had struck him, and suddenly a loud groan escaped his lips. He had recognized the man who still sat motionless behind the steering wheel. It was one of the neighbours.

"He's badly hurt," someone cried.

"Did you hear the way he groaned?"

"He'll have to be moved. He can't stay here."

"There's a chemist's right over there . . ."

Some volunteers seized Trelkovsky by the arms and legs,

to carry him to the chemist's. Two policemen had joined the doctor and were walking with him at the head of the little procession. They laid him out on the prescription counter, hastily swept clean of its normal contents.

"Are you in pain?" the doctor repeated.

He did not answer. He was too preoccupied with the neighbour, who had followed the rest of the group into the store. He saw him go up to one of the policemen and begin talking to him in a confidential murmur.

By this time, the doctor had undertaken a more thorough examination. He straightened up at last, apparently deciding to make public his conclusions.

"You were very lucky," he said. "There's nothing broken. Not even a sprained ankle. All you have, in fact, is a few scratches, and those will be gone in a couple of days. We can take care of them right now. But it was a severe shock; you'll have to stay at home and rest for a while before you're completely recovered."

With the help of the chemist, he covered Trekovsky with mercurochrome and bits of adhesive plaster, and then said, "Naturally, it would be better if you had some X-rays taken, but that isn't urgent. The best thing at the moment is just for you to get as much rest as possible. Where do you live?"

Trelkovsky was terrified. What could he say? But the neighbour spared him the necessity of answering.

"Monsieur lives in the same building I do," he said. "The least I can do for him is to drive him home."

Trelkovsky attempted to sit up and flee, but a score of hands immediately held him back. He went on struggling, but completely uselessly.

"No," he begged. "No, I don't want to go back there with him."

The man smiled down at him as if he were a naughty

child. "Oh, come now," he said. "I'm responsible for what happened to you, and I know it. It's only natural that I should try to make amends. I'll drive you home, and later, when you're better, we can come to some agreement about the damages."

He turned back to the policeman with whom he had been talking earlier. "You won't be needing me any more, officer? You have my name and address?"

The policeman nodded. "You can leave, monsieur. You'll be asked to come in later. And you'll take the responsibility for getting monsieur home?"

"Of course—if you'll just help me to carry him . . ."

Trelkovsky began struggling again. "No," he screamed. "Don't let him take me away! You haven't even taken *my* name and address!"

"Yes, we have," the policeman said. "Monsieur was kind enough to give them to me."

"He's a murderer! He wants to kill me!"

"It's the shock," someone murmured sympathetically.

"He needs sleep," the doctor said. "I'll give him an injection."

"No!" Trelkovsky shouted. "No injections! No shots! They're going to kill me! You've got to stop them; you've got to help me!"

He burst into tears, and his voice trailed off to a pleading whimper. "Please—help me. Take me anywhere, anywhere at all, but don't let them kill me . . ."

They gave him the injection. He felt himself being carried off by men who walked very quickly. He was sleepy. The injection, of course. He wanted to protest, but he had to concentrate all his strength on resisting the impulse to sleep. He was in the car. It was beginning to move.

By an enormous effort of will, he succeeded in not falling asleep. It was as if he were clinging by one hand to the

last rung on the ladder of consciousness. The car was picking up speed. He could make out the driver's back through
the fog that clouded his mind.

And then he thought of the pistol.

He turned over slowly, to free the side pocket in which
he had kept it. His hand was trembling, but it seized the
weapon firmly. He placed its muzzle against the back of
the neighbour's neck.

"Stop this car immediately. I am armed."

The man glanced uneasily at the rear view mirror, and
then burst out laughing.

"Who do you think you could frighten with that?" he
said. "Is it a present for some child?"

Trekovsky pulled frantically at the trigger. Once, twice,
then simply holding it back. The driver's laughter was so
loud in the muffled interior of the car that it seemed inhuman. The tiny bullets from the pistol slapped at his neck
as harmlessly as flies, then bounced off and scattered
across the floor.

"All right—that's enough," the driver croaked. "You
might make me die laughing."

Trelkovsky hurled the pistol at the glass of the wind-
shield. It shattered into little bits of plastic. The driver
turned around and clucked sarcastically.

"Don't cry," he said. "You can buy yourself another
one."

The car slowed down and stopped before the door of
the building. The neighbour got out and slammed the door
behind him. Two of the other neighbours joined him, and
they began a whispered discussion. Trelkovsky just lay in
the back of the car, resigned to his fate, awaiting their
decision. Were they going to execute him immediately?
Somehow, it didn't seem probable.

He realized then that the door on the other side of the

car was not locked, and almost before he knew what he was doing he had seized the handle and leaped into the street. He fell into the arms of a fourth neighbour, who had no trouble mastering him in his semi-drugged condition.

"We're going to carry you up to your apartment," the man told him ironically. 'You'll be able to rest there; and you need a lot of rest. Just lean on me. Don't worry about it—I like to be helpful."

"Let go of me," Trelkovsky shouted. "Let go of me! Help! Help . . ."

A heavy hand laid hard across the side of his face was the only answer he received.

The little group of neighbours now included Monsieur Zy and the concierge. They were all watching him, their eyes gleaming wickedly, making no attempt to conceal their delight.

"But I don't want to go up to my apartment," Trelkovsky said feebly. "I'll give you anything I have, anything you want . . . Just let me go . . ."

The man who was holding him shook his head. "Impossible," he said. "You're going to go quietly upstairs to your apartment. Without making any trouble, or I warn you . . . You know what the doctor said—you need rest, and you're going to get it. You'll see; it will do you good. Now come on, let's go up."

He took Trelkovsky's arm in a thoroughly professional grip, twisted it behind his back and began to press upwards.

"Now, you see, you're already much calmer! You're beginning to understand. That's fine, just go on like that . . . Again, again . . . One step for mama, one for papa, go on . . ."

Step by step Trelkovsky was forced across the threshold, through the entrance hall past the arch that led to the courtyard, and up the steps. The man behind him was still mocking him.

"You didn't want to come with me, eh? Why not? Don't you like your apartment any more? Have you found something else? I thought apartments were scarce these days. But perhaps you made some kind of fake exchange. Well —that's none of my business, after all."

With a final shove, he sent Trelkovsky sprawling on the floor of the front room. The door slammed, and a key turned twice in the lock.

It would undoubtedly be tonight.

17

The Preparations

Trelkovsky struggled painfully to his feet. Every bone and muscle in his body ached. His tongue had discovered a broken tooth and was mechanically attempting to polish its craggy edges. He spit out a slender stream of blood, which kept growing longer and longer as he pushed himself up, stretching from his mouth to the floor, becoming no more than a thread, an imaginary line which refused to break.

The chest of drawers, the armoire, the chairs were all exactly as he had left them at the time of his precipitate flight. He could feel the air coming through the broken window panes. The neighbours had not thought to board them up. They had made a mistake. He dragged himself to the window and inhaled deeply, preparing to scream for help.

He didn't have the time to do it. A torrent of music flooded from every window in the building. The radios had all been turned to maximum volume, and all were playing the Beethoven ninth symphony. He screamed and shouted, but his ineffectual appeals were drowned in the thunder of music. He put his hands to his ears, trying at least to shut out this music he detested so, but even this was in vain. The wind through the courtyard swept it in through the broken panes, filling every corner of the room.

The ninth symphony exploded all around him, bursting with a stupid glee, like the march of the executioners in a comic opera. Nine hundred singers and musicians were exulting in Trelkovsky's approaching death. The neighbours had doubtless considered it a delicate tribute to the memory of Simone Choule, who had been such an admirer of Beethoven. He was swept by a tidal wave of futile rage, and began racing about the apartment, systematically destroying everything that still remained of Simone Choule. First the letters and the books. He tore them apart, reducing all these things that had cast the spell on him to little shreds of paper, scattering them on the floor and then trampling on them.

The impotent fury of an animal caught in a trap seized him by the throat, and he could scarcely breathe. He began hiccuping violently. He went to look for the two incisor teeth in the hole in the wall, but when he got them out and looked at them he saw that they were now two canine teeth. He regarded them for a moment in horror, and then ran back to the window and hurled them out. But as he bent down to throw them as far from him as possible, his attention was caught by the spectacle taking place in the toilet on the other side of the courtyard.

A woman he had never seen before had just come in. She knelt down on the tile floor in front of the bowl, and her head disappeared into its filthy circle. What was she doing? She lifted her head, and there was an expression of utter bestiality on her face. She stared straight at Trelkovsky and smiled repulsively. Then, without taking her eyes from his, she plunged her hand into the toilet bowl, withdrew it filled with excrement and deliberately smeared it across her face. Other women came into the little room, and they all went through the same procedure. When there were thirty or so hideously daubed and smeared women crowded into the toilet a black curtain was drawn across the oval window and he could see nothing more.

Trelkovsky's eyes were fixed and glassy, his lids seemed weighted with lead, he no longer had the strength to flee. He knew that the witches in the room across from him had been sent there to terrify him and drain off his last remaining strength, but he could not escape them. He was too weak, too sick, too worn out.

It was in the courtyard that the rest of the spectacle took place.

A neighbour wearing a workman's blue overalls came in, riding a bicycle. He went all around the court in circles first, and then began cutting back and forth in a figure eight. Each time he passed beneath Trelkovsky's window, he glanced up, smiled broadly and winked. There was a length of cord attached to the seat of the bicycle. The cord was pulling a wax dummy representing a woman. It was the type of mannequin figure used to display dresses in the windows of shops. It leaped and jerked convulsively as it struck against the uneven paving stones, and its arms waved up and down, so that it seemed to be alive. But the wax crumbled rapidly beneath the constant attack of the stones, and the form of the mannequin grew blurred and indistinct. The woman disappeared, as if her flesh had been eaten away by acid. When there were only two legs still trailing behind the bicycle, the neighbour gestured ironically to Trelkovsky and disappeared through the arch.

After him came two men carrying an enormous fish impaled on a pole. They made several circuits of the courtyard before setting down their burden and looking up at

Trelkovsky. Without taking their eyes from his or looking to see what they were doing, even once, they split and gutted the fish. The cast-off entrails piled up until there was a little mound of them on either side of the two men. Then they began laughing delightedly and decorating their hair with them. They formed crowns of the entrails of fish, they hung them from their ears, and draped them around their necks. When they had finished they went off hopping on one foot like young girls playing a game.

One of these same two men reappeared almost immediately. He was blowing into an enormous horn. The sounds he produced resembled those of a giant farting.

A lion wearing a crown then came through the arch. It was obvious that it was nothing more than an old skin concealing two of the neighbours. Riding on the lion was the boy Trelkovsky had seen handing the cape to the executioner on that other night. Two women dressed in white walked across the courtyard to meet the lion. They climbed inside through an opening in the hide, and from the violent contortions of the animal after that Trelkovsky realized that an orgy was taking place beneath the skin. The man with the horn seized the lion by the tail and dragged him out of sight.

Three masked men appeared. Trelkovsky saw with horror that one of the masks clearly resembled his own face. The three men took up positions to form a living picture, but he could not understand what it was meant to be. They remained like that, motionless, for almost an hour. Evening came, and then night and darkness.

The pounding of a horse's hooves echoed from somewhere behind the arch.

Trelkovsky shivered.

Someone was scratching softly at his door.

Already? It wasn't possible. The executioner was just

about to dismount from his horse. A sheet of white paper had been slipped beneath the door, and someone was whispering words he could not make out.

Could someone be coming to his help? Did he possess an ally in the building? He reached for the paper, suspiciously. It was a sheet of perfumed letter paper. He unfolded it carefully. There were just three lines, in a woman's handwriting. He could not decipher what they said. The characters with which the words were formed must have been Sanskrit or Hebrew. He bent down and whispered through the door.

"Who are you?"

There was an answer, but again he could not make out the words. He repeated his question, but all he could hear was a furtive, scurrying sound. Someone must be coming.

And in fact, a few seconds later a key turned in the lock.

18

The Possessed

It was broad daylight when Trelkovsky's body see-sawed across the sill of his window. It crashed through the new glass roof, shattering it into a million tiny shards, and struck the stones of the courtyard in a grotesque position, arms outflung.

He was completely disguised as a woman. The dress, pulled up around his waist by the fall, revealed the outlines of the lace panties and the little rubber fasteners for the stockings. The face was carefully made-up, but the wig had been torn to one side, so that it covered his forehead and his right eye.

The neighbours gathered quickly. The concierge and Monsieur Zy stood at the centre of the group, shaking their heads and gesturing despairingly.

"What an unfortunate young man," Monsieur Zy said. "Yesterday a car accident, and today . . ."

"It's the shock of the accident that caused it!"

"We'll have to call the police emergency squad."

A little later, a police car and an ambulance drew up before the building.

The driver of the police car held out his hand to the landlord, who was an old friend, and said, "You seem to rent all your apartments to suicides."

"Would you believe it?" Monsieur Zy lamented. "And I had just finished repairing the roof!"

The two ambulance attendants were hurriedly unloading their stretcher. There was a doctor with them, and as soon as they were ready all three of them walked over to the motionless body. The doctor shook his head in disgust.

"What kind of a masquerade is this?" he grunted. "He dressed himself up like that to commit suicide?"

Suddenly, as the attendants, the doctor, the policemen and the neighbours watched in stunned bewilderment, the body moved. The mouth opened and a little blood dribbled out. The jaw opened and the mouth said, "It isn't a suicide ... I don't want to die ... It's murder ..."

Monsieur Zy smiled sadly. "The poor young man—he's delirious."

The doctor shook his head again, growing more and more disgusted. "It's a fine time to decide he wants to live. If you want to live, you don't throw yourself out of a vindow."

A trifle more forcefully this time, Trelkovsky's mouth said, "I tell you it was murder ... I was pushed ... I didn't throw myself out of the window ..."

"All right, all right," the doctor agreed. "So it's murder."

The policemen laughed, and one of them said, "He jumped out of the window because he's pregnant."

The doctor apparently did not appreciate this little joke. He signalled to the attendants to lift the body onto the stretcher.

With surprising vigour, Trelkovsky pushed them away. "I forbid you to touch me!" he screamed hysterically. "I am not Simone Choule!"

He managed to stand up, stumbling and shaking, and then seemed to find his balance. The hypnotised spectators dared not intervene.

"You thought everything would happen just the way you wanted it to," he stammered. "You thought my death would be neat and clean. Well, you were wrong. It's going to be filthy, it's going to be horrible! I did not commit suicide. I am not Simone Choule. It was a murder—a hideous murder. Look here, there's the blood!" He paused, and spat on the ground. "That's blood, and I'm dirtying your courtyard with it. I'm not dead yet. You can't kill me that easily!"

He was sobbing like a child now. The doctor and the attendants approached him, moving slowly and awkwardly.

"Come now," the doctor said, "don't make any more trouble. Come on; we're going to take care of you. Just get into the ambulance."

"Don't touch me," Trelkovsky screamed. "I know what you hide behind those white aprons. You disgust me, and your white ambulance disgusts me too. You'll never be able to clean it of the things I'll do to it. You're a gang of murderers! Assassins!"

He started towards the arch that led out of the courtyard, staggering drunkenly. The crowd of neighbours moved aside to form a path for him, staring at him in terror, as if he were a ghost. Alternately laughing and sobbing, Trelkovsky waved his slashed left arm at them, spraying them with blood.

"Did I get you dirty?" he said. "Forgive me—it's my blood, you know. You should have drained the blood first, and then I couldn't have made you dirty now. You forgot that, didn't you?"

The crowd followed him into the entrance hall at a

respectful distance. The policemen looked questioningly at the doctor. Should they subdue him and get him into the ambulance by force? The doctor shook his head.

Blood and tears bubbled together in Trelkovsky's throat. "Just try to stop me from talking!" he screamed. His voice broke, and then came back, on a shriller, higher note. "Murderers! Assassins! I'm really going to make some noise for you now! The kind of scandal you won't forget! And just try to keep me quiet! You can pound on the walls all you like; it doesn't matter to me now!"

He began to spit in every direction, spraying everyone who came too close with a mixture of blood and saliva.

"Murderers! Kill me, just to keep me quiet! But I'll leave something for you to remember; don't think I won't!"

Still staggering he had reached the foot of the staircase. He clutched at the railing and put one foot on the first step. The neighbours had grown a little bolder. They were standing just behind him now.

"Don't come too close, or I'll get all of you dirty!"

He spat at them and they recoiled hastily.

"Be careful, or you'll soil your Sunday clothes! Why don't you go home and put on your red clothes, your working clothes, your murderer's clothes? If you don't, the blood is going to show. And it's hard to get rid of, did you know that? It was easier the last time, wasn't it? But I'm not Simone Choule!"

He had arrived at the first landing. He spat into his open palm and smeared it across the door on the left.

"Assassins! Try to clean that off! It's pretty, isn't it?"

He dragged himself painfully over to the door on the right, rubbed his bleeding arm across its surface, and then spat on the doorknob. A piece of a tooth fell out of his mouth.

"Ah!" he shouted. "That's fine! You'll have a nice tidy place now!"

The neighbours were climbing the steps behind him, beginning to let out a threatening rumble of voices. He tore off the upper part of the dress and scraped his fingernails violently across his chest. Blood began to pour from the wound. He gathered some of it into his left hand and shook it from his fingers over the door mat.

"You'll have to change your door mat now. You can never remove blood stains!"

He fell to his hands and knees to climb to the second landing, leaving a trail of blood on the steps.

"You'll have to change the staircase too—there's blood on that. You'll never be able to clean away all this blood!"

One of the neighbours managed to reach through the railing and grasp his foot, attempting to pull him back.

"Get your hands off me, murderer!" He hissed like an angry cat and spat full in the man's face. The neighbour released his foot and clasped both his hands to his face.

Trelkovsky laughed. "If you wipe at it like that, you'll have it all over you. Who would like some blood? What? No one? But you eat your steaks bloody rare, you love rabbit stewed in its own blood, you know which shops have the best blood sausage, and you worship the blood of the Lord, don't you? Then why don't you want some of Trelkovsky's good blood?"

On the second landing, he smeared both of the doors with blood and saliva, just as he had on the first.

The policemen had brought out their clubs and were clutching them in their hands, in spite of the doctor's order. They were obviously just waiting their chance to strike out at this madman, this creature possessed by devils, and silence him once and for all. But the crush of neighbours in the narrow staircase blocked their passage and prevented them from intervening. They tried to push through them, but the neighbours refused to budge. They were muttering angrily now, showing their teeth. The doctor and the attendants got no further than the police. They had no real desire to take part in this painful comedy, so they simply stopped where they were and began exchanging their impressions of it all with the policemen. On the third landing, the neighbours had surrounded Trelkovsky. Gleaming instruments shone in their hands. Instruments with razor-edged blades, like those in an operating room. They pushed Trelkovsky through the door of his apartment.

"So!" he said, "you do like blood, after all! Where is Monsieur Zy? Ah, there he is ... Come on, come on Monsieur Zy—you don't want to miss getting your share. And the concierge? A lovely morning, isn't it, madame? And Madame Dioz, I see you've come to collect your pint of blood!"

He burst out in a spasm of demented laughter. The instruments glistened in the hands of the neighbours. A streamer of blood raced across his abdomen ...

For the second time, Trelkovsky's body see-sawed across the window sill, and crashed through the debris of the glass roof into the courtyard.

Epilogue

Trelkovsky was not dead, not yet.

He emerged very slowly from a bottomless abyss. And as he recovered consciousness he became aware again of his body, could feel its pain. It seemed to come from everywhere, from every direction at once, hurling itself at him like a mad dog. He knew he would never be able to protect himself. He was prepared to admit defeat, but his own resistance surprised him. The pain persisted, and then, wave after wave, it drew back and at last disappeared completely.

He fell asleep, exhausted by the struggle. He was awakened by the sound of voices.

"She has come out of the coma."

"She may still have a chance."

"After what she's gone through, it would really be a chance!"

"Did you know that they used the whole of the blood reserve for her?"

Gently, with infinite precaution, he opened one eye. He could make out a blurred group of silhouettes. White shadows moving back and forth in a white room. He must be in a hospital. But who was it the silhouettes were talking about?

"She lost an enormous amount of blood. It's a good thing it isn't a rare type. If it were ..."

"We'll have to raise the leg a little bit more. She'll be more comfortable."

He sensed that someone or something was pulling at one of his limbs, very far from him, miles away. And he did feel more comfortable. Then these phrases he had overheard—they were talking about him! But why would they speak of him as if he were a woman?

He thought about it for a long time. He had great difficulty gathering his thoughts into any sort of concrete form. Sometimes he went on thinking without being able to remember what he was thinking about. His brain turned endlessly around a void, and then it began to come back to him, he began to pick up the threads of his own reason.

He supposed that they were mocking him. They continued to talk about him as if he were a woman because of the way he had been dressed. They were ridiculing him, in defiance of all justice. He detested them so violently that his vision blurred again. A wave of nervous trembling swept through his body, reawakening the dormant pain. He let himself slip off in a tide of suffering.

Later on, he felt somewhat better. He was in another white room now, much larger than the one he had been in before. It was still impossible for him to move. In the little angle of vision he possessed, he could just catch glimpses of other beds containing other recumbent forms. Then, quite suddenly, the room was filled with men and women, scattering among all the beds.

Someone walked up, very close to him, and he heard the rustling of paper. Whoever it was had placed a package on the night table to the left of the bed. He saw the man when he sat down.

He was undoubtedly delirious. It was fortunate that he was conscious of this fact, or his mind might have gone completely. Feature for feature, the man was his double. It was another Trelkovsky who was seated at his bedside, silent and mournful. He wondered whether there really was a man sitting there, transformed by his fever into a living replica of himself, or whether the whole apparition was simply an invention of his tortured brain. He felt suddenly disposed to study this problem. The pain had practically disappeared. He was floating in a downy vacuum that was not at all disagreeable. It was almost as if he had accidentally discovered some secret form of balance. Far from terrifying him, the vision had reassured him. The image he had seen was like a reflection in a mirror, and in that way it was comforting. He yearned to see himself like that in a mirror.

He heard the sound of whispering voices, and then a head was abruptly framed in his field of vision. He recognised that face at once; it was Stella. Her mouth was pulled back in a smile that revealed two canine teeth of abnormal size, and she was speaking slowly, as though she had trouble understanding the language she used.

"Simone, Simone," she was saying, "you recognize me, don't you? It's Stella; your friend, Stella. Don't you recognize me?"

A moaning sound came from Trelkovsky's mouth, stifled at first, then swelling to an unbearable scream.